WHERE ALL GOOD
FLAPPERS GO

To Mildred Scott Earle, aka Topsy (1902–1991),
the original flapper grandmother, and to
Lauren, who now wears her ring.

WHERE ALL GOOD FLAPPERS GO

Essential Stories of the Jazz Age

Selected and introduced by
David M. Earle

PUSHKIN PRESS

LONDON

Pushkin Press
Somerset House, Strand
London WC2R 1LA

First published by Pushkin Press in 2023

1 3 5 7 9 8 6 4 2

ISBN 13: 978-1-78227-930-3

Designed and typeset by Tetragon, London
Printed and bound by TJ Books

www.pushkinpress.com

CONTENTS

Introduction

The flapper is perhaps the most instantly recognizable figure of 1920s America, which is why it is surprising that this is the first anthology of stories dedicated to her. She was a controversial embodiment of modernity, of shifting gender norms, and the break with earlier codes of behavior. She symbolized all the newness of the post-WWI generation, of the age of Prohibition, jazz, speakeasies, motor cars, and mobility.

The term "flapper" was initially British theatrical slang for young girls, especially those who gushed over matinée idols. By 1912, it was being used in America to describe modish girls who wore the new style of non-girdled, low waisted dresses, tended toward slimness, and were heavily made up. By the end of the war, as soldiers returned, hemlines rose farther, and jazz's popularity spread across the country, the "flapper" came to signify the young generation's post-war mixture of jaded optimism and high energy.

Unlike the suffragettes before them, flappers were more interested in social and sexual equality than political. They traded the long hair, wasp waists, and corsets of the Edwardian Gibson Girl, so well suited for the drawing room, for bobbed hair, simple short dresses with rolled stockings that exposed the ankle and knee, and a straight boyish profile. This new style celebrated the speed and mobility of modern life and broke with the cumbersome expectations of the stay-at-home wife and mother-to-be. Flapper fashion was at one with the flapper's lifestyle, which advocated for life on the same terms as their male counterparts (known as "flippers" or, later, "sheiks"). Why, the flapper demanded, weren't women allowed to listen to jazz, drink, smoke, and be sexually active—at least active enough to "park and pet."

From the late 1910s, more and more women enrolled in college and trade schools, the boom economy created a high demand for office workers and shop girls, and women migrated to cities and were able to support themselves (almost all of these stories take place in New York City, America's capital of modernity). The flapper's advocacy for social and sexual equality appealed to this new class of urban woman. But these expanding roles for women and the unregulated intermingling of the sexes in the urban spaces and on campuses created a certain amount of anxiety for the more conservative elements who saw flapperdom as evidence of the decline of American morality. This fear was only compounded by the 1920s fascination with youth culture and by prohibition—the speakeasy removed restrictions against the separation of gender, class, and even race.

As was true of the 1920s, the flapper phenomenon was neither simple nor homogeneous. This decade saw widespread and often violent division: Jim Crow racism, economic inflation and disparity, and tectonic shifts in mores and social behavior. The definition of the flapper itself changed over the decade and registered many of these turbulent aspects; so too do these stories. Herein you will find many of the tropes that have become synonymous with flapperdom: the heroine of "Clever Little Fool" struggling to balance her fast lifestyle with the expectations of marriage; a shy girl's transformation into a flirtatious flapper by adopting snappy dialogue in "Bernice Bobs Her Hair"; the aviatrix in "The Bride of Ballyhoo" using performance and spectacle to further her career; a powder-room attendant in "Night Club" embodying the tensions between the older generations and younger. Yet these stories are far from univocal. Authors including Dorothy Parker, Anita Loos, and Viña Delmar skewer preconceptions of the flapper even as they rely upon them. Dawn Powell's "Not the Marrying Kind" inverts and updates the romance formula for the modern girl just as the main character of "Something for Nothing" inverts the idea of urban sophistication; gold-diggers and chorus girls—extreme manifestations of flapperdom—appear in stories by African American authors, like "The Chicago Kid" and "Monkey Junk," which make evident the decade's wealth disparity and limited options for women—especially African American women. Whereas the flapper movement is largely and reductively identified with the white middle class, it drew inspiration from the jazz culture and the perceived joyousness of African American society, just then reaching its renaissance in Harlem, and the presence of blackness can be found submerged in many of these stories (not always positively) by white authors. (Indeed, the flapper movement's proximity to black culture via jazz added to the larger white fear of cultural degradation.)

The flapper was a figure of both fascination and fear, of feminine empowerment and risqué sexuality, as the many chorus girls and gold-diggers in flapper fiction illustrate. She was debated from pulpit to press—but appeared nowhere more frequently than in the magazines of the day. By all accounts the 1920s were "magazine crazy," with magazines catering to every interest and social position. The flapper's merits were debated in middle-class magazines like the *Saturday Evening Post*, which had a circulation over 2,000,000 and helped propel F. Scott Fitzgerald to stardom. Her high-society position and fashion was glamorized in women's magazines, which Anita Loos ironically lampoons here in "Why Girls Go South," originally published in *Harper's Bazaar*. She was championed in magazines like *College Humor*, which captured the fast quip- and slang-laden dialogue of youth culture (and which Dorothy Parker's "Mantle of Whistle" hilariously sends up), and in the working-class pulp magazines, such as *Snappy Stories* which provides five of the thirteen stories in this collection and launched the careers of Dawn Powell, Katharine Brush, and Viña Delmar. These light, entertaining, mildly risqué stories were the reading material for those same typists, stenographers and shop girls who saw themselves reflected in the magazine's working-class heroines even while their fantasies of upward mobility were enacted by the many high-society heroines as well. The importance of these magazines can be seen in stories like Delmar's "Thou Shalt Not Killjoy" where a naughty pulp magazine demolishes the hold nineteenth-century morality has on the flapper's prissy love interest.

Unfortunately, there were no pulp magazines for African Americans, so flapper fiction for a black audience and by black authors like Gertrude Schalk, Rudolph Fisher, and Zora Neale Hurston, all represented here, was published in black newspapers like the *Pittsburgh Courier* and the *National News*, illustrating the important but often overlooked inter-relationships between African American culture and white flapperdom.

With this collection, the largely lost genre of popular fiction that defined the flapper in the popular consciousness of the 1920s is brought vividly back to life, as is the flapper herself—complex, unapologetic, and as jazzy as ever.

WHAT BECAME
OF THE FLAPPERS?

Zelda Fitzgerald

McCall's, October 1925

FLAPPER WASN'T a particularly fortunate cognomen. It is far too reminiscent of open galoshes and covered up cars and all other proverbial flapper paraphernalia, which might have passed unnoticed save for the name. All these things are—or were—amusing externals of a large class of females who in no way deserve the distinction of being called flappers. The flappers that I am writing this article about are a very different and intriguing lot of young people who are perhaps unstable, but who are giving us the first evidence of youth asserting itself out of the cradle. They are not originating new ideas or new customs or new moral standards. They are simply endowing the old ones that we are used to with a vitality that we are not used to. We are not accustomed to having *our* daughters think our ideas for themselves, and it is distasteful to some of us that we are no longer able to fit the younger generation into our conceptions of what the younger generation was going to be like when we watched it in the nursery. I do not think that anything my daughter could possibly do eighteen years from now would surprise me. And yet I will probably be forbidding her in frigid tones to fly more than three thousand feet high or more than five hundred miles an hour with little Willie Jones, and bidding her never to go near that horrible Mars. I can imagine these things now, but if they should happen twenty years from now, I would certainly wonder what particular dog my child was going to…

The flapper springs full-grown, like Minerva, from the head of her once déclassé father, Jazz, upon whom she lavishes affection and reverence, and deepest filial regard. She is not a "condition arisen from war unrest," as I have so often read in the shower of recent praise and protest which she has evoked, and to which I am contributing. She is a direct result of the greater appreciation of beauty, youth, gaiety, and grace which is sweeping along in a carmagnole (I saw one in a movie once, and I use this word advisedly) with our young anti-puritans at the head. They have placed such a premium on the flapper creed—to give and get amusement—that even the dumb-bells become Dulcies and convert stupidity into charm. Dulcy is infinitely preferable to the kind of girl who, ten years ago, quoted the Rubaiyat at you and told you how misunderstood she was; or the kind who straightened your tie as evidence that in her lay the spirit of the eternal mother; or the kind who spent long summer evenings telling you that it wasn't the *number* of cigarettes you smoked that she minded but just the *principle*, to show off her nobility of character. These are some of the bores of yesterday. Now even bores must be original, so the more unfortunate members of the flapper sect have each culled an individual line from their daily rounds, which amuses or not according to whether you have seen the same plays, heard the same tunes or read reviews of the same books.

The best flapper is reticent emotionally and courageous morally. You always know what she thinks, but she does all her feeling alone. These are two characteristics which will bring social intercourse to a more charming and sophisticated level. I believe in the flapper as an involuntary and invaluable cupbearer to the arts. I believe in the flapper as an artist in her particular field, the art of being—being young, being lovely, being an object.

For almost the first time, we are developing a class of pretty yet respectable young women, whose sole functions are to amuse and to make growing old a more enjoyable process for some men and staying young an easier one for others.

Even parents have ceased to look upon their children as permanent institutions. The fashionable mother no longer keeps her children young so that she will preserve the appearance of a debutante. She helps them to mature so that she will be mistaken for a stepmother. Once her girls are old enough to be out of finishing school, a period of freedom and social activity sets in for her. The daughters are rushed home to make a chaotic début and embark upon a feverish chase for a husband. It is no longer permissible to be single at twenty-five. The flapper makes haste to marry lest she be a leftover and be forced to annex herself to the crowd just younger. She hasn't time to ascertain the degree of compatibility between herself and her fiancé before the wedding, so she ascertains that they will be separated if the compatibility should be mutually rated zero after it.

The flapper! She is growing old. She forgets her flapper creed and is conscious only of her flapper self. She is married 'mid loud acclamation on the part of relatives and friends. She has come to none of the predicted "bad ends," but has gone at last, where all good flappers go—into the young married set, into boredom and gathering conventions and the pleasure of having children, having lent a while a splendor and courageousness and brightness to life, as all good flappers should.

THE CLEVER
LITTLE FOOL

Dana Ames

Snappy Stories, June 15th 1926

MARGIE KNIGHT was admittedly a fool—but a clever one. She was the mothers' menace type of girl, if you know what I mean. "What I want to know is—what kind of children will a girl like that have? Tell me that!" And, "It's not that I can't trust my son Albert. He has a remarkably strong will power, but—" And, "Of course I can't see anything so attractive about her, she's just *noisy*—"

All of which means that Margie was a cute little thing with the kind of nose that Gloria Swanson has made famous, and a mop of gold-red hair that crinkled a bit.

She was, in type, the perennial flapper, and undoubtedly she might have gone on for five years slithering across the dancing floor of the Gates' End Country Club, and in the same fashion trudging over its links, and motoring speedily along the smooth boulevards that led to it and more especially away from it. She managed to be mildly crazy about two or three men at a time, with an occasional college boy thrown in during vacations. A fairly good line she had, too.

"Listen… you can't expect me to believe *that*?"

"Well, after all, you *are* so good looking and popular and everything, and somebody told me somep'n about you once! You've got a perfectly terrible reputation—"

"Listen, it's not that I don't trust you absolutely, but my conscience is non-skid—"

Yes, a fairly good line. Margie was a little fool, of course, but a rather clever one, at that.

And, at nineteen, she looked back over the many and varied experiences she'd gone through since she had left Miss Gulliver's School two years before, and found them good. She wasn't half so sophisticated as she thought she was—nobody could be—but her assumption of ennui, remembered hastily in moments of super-jazz, was most captivating.

She might have gone on five years, easily, broadcasting thrills without a pause for intensive thought at the Gates' End Country Club—if she hadn't found the White Hair.

The finding of the White Hair was brought about in the most casual, ordinary way. It was two-thirty in the afternoon, and Margie was bellowing from her bedroom for the immediate services of one black and affable Cora. Cora was shared between Margie, her mother, and an older sister, and it is quite possible that Cora worked harder upstairs than the cook ever did downstairs. However...

Margie was due for a game of golf at the country club at three. At two-thirty, therefore, Cora was helping her into an athletic undergarment of turquoise silk, beige woolen stockings and swagger little oxfords with suede fringes. Margie, leaping to the dresser to powder her nose, was all ready except for the sweater and skirt that Cora was patiently dangling in mid-air.

"Nev' mind, Cora darling, I'll just drag a comb through the old haystack and jump into the clothes—dee-ump-dump-dump—deum-dump-dump—Oh-h!-o-h!—OH!"

"Too many gin fizzes 'fore lunch and your nerves are all jumpy," Cora remarked sagely. "Here, honey, lemme—"

But Margie was standing practically petrified, holding gingerly between thumb and forefinger an authentic White Hair. Fifteen minutes later she tottered weakly to the phone and informed Jimmy Nesbit that she couldn't possibly play golf until further notice.

Of course she shouldn't have taken the thing so seriously. But think of the things in this odd little world that are taken seriously, if it comes to that.

"It isn't the fact that I've had a white hair," she remarked plaintively to her mother. "'Cause Lord knows I pulled that one out faster'n the eye could see! But any day I might find another—and another—and another!"

Soberly she stared into the picture of her complete decay. She saw herself with twinges of rheumatism in her dancing legs—with pouches under her very blue eyes—with natural bracelets around her slim white throat.

Just as soberly she jerked out of the turquoise blue thing and the woolly sweater and skirt, and allowed herself to be poured into a warm tub with the right kind of bath salts for evening and likewise into a ginger-colored georgette dinner dress. Then she treated Jimmy Nesbit to three or four of her father's drinks, snatched from the paneled safe under the sideboard in the dining room—Margie having cracked harder propositions than safes in her time. And so, as Mr. Pepys says, on her rather mournful way with Jimmy Nesbit to the Country Club...

The Older Generation—playfully called "older" not because of the way they looked but because of the way they wore their inhibitions—had long since given up coming to the club in the evenings. They patronized the links and timidly they sat on the wide, awninged veranda in the afternoons, but it was understood that their sons and daughters disapproved heartily of their making themselves conspicuous after 10 p.m. They were expected to motor into town for the Opera, a calm and cruel dictate to which they bowed their heads, meekly.

Consequently the Gates' End ballroom looked, as Margie and Jimmy paraded into it, like a Methodist minister's idea of the devil's own go-cart, rapidly sliding southward.

"H'lo! H'lo there, Margie! Come and get a little nip right out of daddy's hip pocket—"

"Say, Margie, come and Charleston with me after I get through tossing Jim Nesbit outa window. I'm sick and tired of this girl Peggy snagging her heels in my instep—"

Margie snapped automatically into form. It was all right for Bill Older to kid Peggy Carruthers, because everybody knew that Peggy turned down his honorable proposal of matrimony every weekend. And everybody knew, too, that no one could Charleston the way Margie could Charleston.

She grinned, and slid into Jimmy's arms. After one dance they skidded into a locker room and had many drinks from many flasks. Quiet, sweet little drinks. The whole gang was there, howling and purring and screeching just as usual. And, as far as these things can be rated outside of the novels of 1910, Margie was the star of the performance—also as usual. There wasn't any dead hush when she came into a room, or anything medieval like that, but there were a dozen proffered drinks, dances, dates or whatever anybody happened to have. Life ought to have been a pleasant bonbon for Margie Knight... it *ought* to have been.

She drifted out to a corner of the veranda for a little judicious necking with Jimmy. Jimmy was her current heavy love. He hadn't been last week, and he might not be next week, but he was now.

"Gosh! What a night!" said Jimmy.

Margie sighed. She recognized this as the opening of the Line Romantic.

But she murmured, "Umm-h'mm—stars 'n—'n the moon 'n everything."

"Sure. Listen, did anyone ever tell you—"

Margie sighed again, almost inaudibly, her mind on other matters. Jimmy was a sweet kid, but meaningless. He'd just come out of Princeton with a great gesture, aged twenty-two years and eight months. And it was well known that, just as he'd contracted with his father not to smoke until he was eighteen, so had he contracted not to marry until he was twenty-five. At the risk of losing most of the mint and a handful of railroads.

Looking back over her heavy loves, Margie admitted ruefully to herself that there had been something the matter with all of them… if one considered them matrimonially. One had a wife—a sort of a wife—another was too pouchy around the eyes, another subsisted solely as a perennial house guest, another—

Oh, Lord! What was the use! Wasn't there *anything* hanging around loose for a girl to marry!

There was not. And Margie, since she'd found the White Hair, was determined that she must marry while her market value was at its height. She just couldn't go on having a good time until she joined the rocking chair brigade—still with a one-syllable prefix hitched to her name. This might be 1926—but that sort of thing wasn't done. You simply had to be "one of our prettiest debutantes" or else "one of the most popular of our younger matrons." And you couldn't go on being one of our prettiest debutantes with silver threads among the gold—not in this day of being quick on the hip and fast on the draught.

But Jimmy was still talking.

"Honestly, I never knew a girl I was so crazy about. You've got just simply everything, Margie. Looks and charm—and all the manly virtues. You know what I mean. Carrying your alcohol and not blowing lady-like smoke rings and all that. There's always been something that's got me on the ragged edge about every woman I've ever known—except you."

"Oh, gosh, Jimmy—I get so sort of fed up! What good does it do me being marvelous? What good does it do any of us? If we were really knockouts—Peggy Joyce or Gilda Gray or the Queen of Roumania—you see what I mean? I'm not really marvelous at all, that's just moonlight and moonshine—I'm just what's called a 'good egg' and also in the interesting process of either getting scrambled or hard-boiled."

"You're morbid tonight."

Margie lit a cigarette and tossed the match to the lawn. "No, I only just stopped pulling a line, for once. And consequently you get scared to death of me. Nev' mind, Jimmy dear. Let's go inside and show 'em all how two white people can dance when they really want to."

But this wasn't the end of that particular evening on the profane precincts of the Gates' End Country Club—not by a long way.

Margie, being a good egg whether she wanted to be or not, was not one to leave an evening flat on its back, strangling for breath. Nor did anyone but the dumb Jimmy have any inkling that there was anything preying on what might have been her mind. She didn't get up and announce to the assembled throng that frankly she wanted a husband and that she wouldn't be happy till she got one—with a single chin and six bank accounts. She kept on dancing without a pause if you don't count the glides into the locker room from time to time—until it was about one o'clock and the black boy with the banjo was just getting good—and Janet Prescott came in with a new man on her arm.

Immediately Margie spotted the new man, and bore down on him, figuratively. It looked as if Heaven had suddenly taken a great personal interest in Margie. For it was whispered around, faster than a six-tube set could broadcast an Indian love lyric, that this new man, by name of Robert Luther, was thirty years old, unattached as a floating pink cloud, and just delirious with money.

And Robert fell for Margie.

They went out on the veranda. (A different corner from the last time—Margie had her subtle delicacies.)

And to Margie's infinite satisfaction, Robert not only went in straightway for the Line Romantic but likewise for the Line Protective. From which you can always distinguish the men who marry from the men who like to have their breakfasts alone with a siphon bottle.

"Sure you won't be cold? That dress—"

Margie preened in ginger-color. "Don't you like the dress?"

"H'mm... it's a pretty shade, but if you belonged to me—"

Margie shook the mop of red-gold hair out of her eyes. "I don't like it very much myself. It's too—too extreme. But you've no idea how hard it is—to sort of keep up with the—the others—"

He slipped an arm around her shoulders. "You don't mind, Margie? If you were my own sister—I wish, though, you'd let me tell you what I think about you?"

"I'd adore having you..."

"Well, even in just this half hour of our knowing each other, I think probably I understand you a lot better than all these friends of yours do. They're trying to make a jazz-girl out of you, and all the time you're the mother type."

Margie restrained her little heels from kicking. "I—I'd like to live up to your ideal of me, but honestly I'm just a silly little thing—"

"Oh—no! D'you mind if I kiss you, just once?"

This was a poser. Up to this time Margie had hated men who put any responsibility up to anybody but themselves. But she kind of turned her cheek around. Robert Luther kissed her. Chastely.

When they finally got back into the big room, Margie was worrying over whether to have Janet Prescott or Alice Dorn for maid of honor. Robert's intentions, seething in his mind, were as evident as the Star Spangled Banner on the Fourth of July...

Obviously it was her cue now to be demure, and Margie Knight was not one to miss a cue. It was hard, though, seeing Janet in the limelight, clad scantily in the leopard-skin rug off the tiles in front of the fireplace, doing an imitation of somebody or other doing something.

"Oh, *fine*!" said Jimmy, cattily. "Here we have a moving picture, vintage of 1908—"

Jimmy was jealous on Margie's account, because Margie and Janet had always been rivals for the calcium glow...

But Margie didn't mind, this time—much. Because Robert Luther evidently wasn't aware that there was a girl in a leopard-skin garment alive in the world. His nice brown eyes were as fixed on Margie as tacks in a carpet. They had, off in the locker room, two nice little drinks of straight lemonade with seltzer water (Margie giving occasional little squeaks because it was so sizzy!) and while they were indulging in these refreshments Robert told her All About Himself.

"I just know you come from the West," said Margie.

"Say, that's clever of you. Yes, Wyoming, and I only came East to round off a cattle deal; I can't always trust my agents in New York for the big stuff. They're terribly afraid of turning over five cents—"

Margie's eyes were admiring. Golly! How she *did* need, with her tastes, the sort of husband who wasn't afraid of turning over five cents! Yea, verily…

"I honestly think you're simply wonderful," she said, with a certain earnestness.

"Oh, I don't know! Just business. But I'm sure talking about business must be dull for you. My kid sister—she's the one who married Jordan Arthur, the bread king—well, she always says when I get started on cattle I'm impossible. By the way, I want you to meet my sister some time soon. She's keen to have me marry some attractive, really decent girl—and settle down—"

Decent? Margie wondered. What were the Wyoming standards of decency, anyhow? It made so much difference whether or no you had a decent *mind*. Some people might think that she and Jimmy Nesbit, two nights ago, had been—had been, well, a little reckless. But Margie thought then, and still thought now, that when you're young and very much alive and the stars are out like a thousand million diamonds—well, that you can't be expected to act as if you had wrinkles behind the ears.

Wrinkles. White Hair. Age. Security.

That brought her back, fast enough, to Robert Luther. She leaned forward a little, and in a moment she was in his arms. Not much thrill to Robert, but he was darn nice. Anybody could see that. Treated her as if she were eighteenth century lace. Now Jimmy always treated her, when he got the chance, as if she were sport flannel, washable… and absolutely nothing by the yard! Margie gave herself a little mental shake. It wasn't quite square reconciling herself to a new love by running down an old one.

"Say!" said Robert suddenly. "I'm going to run back to the hotel and get some pictures I have of my sister and her family. I want to show you. I'll be back in half an hour."

Margie waved goodbye to Robert and sauntered into the big room. She was radiant, but a little thoughtful too. A man doesn't dash off in the middle of the night to show you pictures of his sister unless he's as serious as pneumonia. Margie knew that. She *had* Mr. Robert Luther. And forthwith she would become "one of our most popular young matrons" any time she wanted. She could easily persuade Robert to live in the East, while he was in the first wild transports or whatever you called 'em—and probably Janet Prescott had better be maid-of-honor—.

Well, this was her last half hour, then, of being wild. She shook off her conscience and made a dash for Jimmy.

"It's too bad," he said grumpily "that a guy can't see the girl he dragged to a rotten dance more'n once every four hours—"

"Not a rotten dance. Listen to that music!" Margie flashed a grin at the black boy with the banjo. "Listen—he's playing somep'n *good*. Don't know what it is, but they wrote it on molasses."

Jimmy was immediately in a good humor. That was one of the nice things about Jimmy. He didn't have any sense.

"Sure is keen music. Keen time, too. And a keen dress you got on."

"Like it?"

"Sure do. Always like economy. Every time I see an economical girl I say, *'There's* a woman for a white man to love.'"

"You're such a sil', Jimmy."

"Sure. So are you. Only clever. I understand you perfectly."

"Sometimes I think you do, too, Jimmy."

"I *know* it. I can imagine all the things you do when I'm not around. Try me."

"All right! What do I like for breakfast?"

"Easy. A gin fizz, toast, marmalade and strong black coffee. Right?"

"Absolutely. How did you know?"

"Because that's my idea of a morning meal. And we're sisters under the sex… Go on, what else do you want to know?"

"Well, Jimmy, what kind of people am I politest to?"

"Servants."

"Bulls' eye!"

"Sure."

"Now, then—not counting you in on this—what's my idea of morality?"

"Matter of mood and man with you, generally. But you'd never be emotionally sloppy. If you ever got in any kind of a jam, you wouldn't have hysterics. You'd have a cold bath, and think it over on a cigarette."

"You darling!"

"Sure."

"Listen, I can't tell you why—but I want you to kiss me now—immediately!"

Affably Jimmy took her elbow and they slithered out to the jaded veranda.

He kissed her.

Then Robert came back. Margie remembered nervously all about the Future—you can remember about the Future, you know. And Robert looked so nice and protective and clean-cut and all that.

Margie tripped from Jimmy to Robert.

Robert took her quite out of earshot of the saxophone, always a favorable sign, because a saxophone is the patron saint of love affairs, not marriages.

"As I was saying," said Robert, quite as if he hadn't been away at all, "I think I understand you. Perfectly. And I've been thinking it over during my drive. Fact is,

Margie—dear—I want a wife. I want to get married. Settle down. Have kiddies."

"Well—except maybe for just over the weekends—"

Robert didn't hear this mild and flippant interruption. "Will you be my wife?" he said.

Here it was. Away with the Menace of the White Hair! Here was a man with looks and money and family. And she was nineteen.

"See," said Robert Luther, suddenly, diving into an inner pocket. He was one of those men who keep things in inner pockets. "See, here's my kid sister at Miami—"

This sister-in-law of hers was evidently going to play an important part in her life. Margie looked with mild interest at the snapshot of a pretty girl in a bathing suit.

"Nice—very nice," she said.

"Oh yes," said Robert. "That one was taken—let's see—that was taken summer before she was married. Just after she finished boarding school. Now *this* one shows her with her husband and the kids—that's all I've got of her—"

Casually Margie took the picture from his hand. Casually—at first—she searched for the face of the pretty girl...

A worried looking young woman in a ghastly motor outfit. A masterful man with a cigar, standing by her side. Three small and mad looking children scowling in the sun.

"They travel all over the country together in an automobile," Robert remarked with satisfaction. "Jordan's crazy about motoring. But they lead the most well-regulated lives of any people I know. Before they were married Jordan said to me, 'I'll take *care* of Cynthia because I *understand* Cynthia,' and that's the——"

But that was as far as he got. Because Margie had fled.

When he saw her again Margie and Jimmy Nesbit were celebrating, for no reason at all, the Fall of the Bastille. And then Margie was shrieking with mirth.

"Listen, gang! I've got a White Hair! See—find it for 'em, Jimmy!" (Margie had forgotten pulling that lorn hair out.) "I'm going in for one of those distinguished white streaks that duchesses have—won't it be gorgeous?"

"How exciting!" cried Janet Prescott, not without a tinge of envy. Margie was always thinking up something extraordinary.

"Yes, I think so," said Margie, biting Jimmy's ear. "I thought it was terrible at first, but after this and from now on I'm going in for being myself. *You* know, Jimmy——"

BERNICE BOBS HER HAIR

F. Scott Fitzgerald

Saturday Evening Post, May 1st 1920

I

AFTER DARK on Saturday night one could stand on the first tee of the golf course and see the country club windows as a yellow expanse over a very black and wavy ocean. The waves of this ocean, so to speak, were the heads of many curious caddies, a few of the more ingenious chauffeurs, the golf professional's deaf sister—and there were usually several stray, diffident waves who might have rolled inside had they so desired. This was the gallery.

The balcony was inside. It consisted of the circle of wicker chairs that lined the wall of the combination club-room and ballroom. At these Saturday-night dances it was largely feminine; a great babel of middle-aged ladies with sharp eyes and icy hearts behind lorgnettes and large bosoms. The main function of the balcony was critical, it occasionally showed grudging admiration, but never approval, for it is well known among ladies over thirty-five that when the younger set dance in the summer time it is with the very worst intentions in the world, and if they are not bombarded with stony eyes stray couples will dance weird barbaric interludes in the corners, and the more popular, more dangerous girls will sometimes be kissed in the parked limousines of unsuspecting dowagers.

But, after all, this critical circle is not close enough to the stage to see the actors' faces and catch the subtler byplay. It can only frown and lean, ask questions and make satisfactory deductions from its set of postulates, such as the one which states that every young man with a large income leads the life of a hunted partridge. It never really appreciates the drama of the shifting, semi-cruel world of adolescence. No; boxes, orchestra circle, principals, and chorus are represented by the medley of faces and voices that sway to the plaintive African rhythm of Dyer's dance orchestra.

From sixteen-year-old Otis Ormonde, who has two more years at Hill School, to G. Reece Stoddard, over whose bureau at home hangs a Harvard law diploma; from little Madeleine Hogue, whose hair still feels strange and uncomfortable on top of her head, to Bessie MacRae, who has been the life of the party a little too long—more than ten years—the medley is not only the center of the stage but contains the only people capable of getting an unobstructed view of it.

With a flourish and a bang the music stops. The couples exchange artificial, effortless smiles, facetiously repeat "*la*-de-*da*-*da* dum*dum*," and then the clatter of young feminine voices soars over the burst of clapping.

A few disappointed stags caught in midfloor as they had been about to cut in subsided listlessly back to the walls, because this was not like the riotous Christmas dances. These summer hops were considered just pleasantly warm and exciting, where even the younger marrieds rose and performed ancient waltzes and terrifying fox trots to the tolerant amusement of their younger brothers and sisters.

Warren McIntyre, who casually attended Yale, being one of the unfortunate stags, felt in his dinner-coat pocket for a cigarette and strolled out onto the wide, semi-dark veranda, where couples were scattered at tables, filling the lantern-hung night with vague words and hazy laughter. He nodded here and there at the less absorbed and as he passed each couple some half-forgotten fragment of a story played in his mind, for it was not a large city and every one was Who's Who to everyone else's past. There, for example, were Jim Strain and Ethel Demorest, who had been privately engaged for three years. Everyone knew that as soon as Jim managed to hold a job for more than two months she would marry him. Yet how bored they both looked, and how wearily Ethel regarded Jim sometimes, as if she wondered why she had trained the vines of her affection on such a wind-shaken poplar.

Warren was nineteen and rather pitying with those of his friends who hadn't gone East to college. But, like most boys, he bragged tremendously about the girls of his city when he was away from it. There was Genevieve Ormonde, who regularly made the rounds of dances, house parties, and football games at Princeton, Yale, Williams and Cornell; there was black-eyed Roberta Dillon, who was quite as famous to her own generation as Hiram Johnson or Ty Cobb; and, of course, there was Marjorie Harvey, who besides having a fairylike face and a dazzling, bewildering tongue was already justly celebrated for having turned five cart wheels in succession during the last pump-and-slipper dance at New Haven.

Warren, who had grown up across the street from Marjorie, had long been wildly in love with her. Sometimes she seemed to reciprocate his feeling with a faint gratitude, but she had tried him by her infallible test and informed him gravely that she did not love him. Her test was that when she was away from him she forgot him and had affairs with other boys. Warren found this discouraging, especially as Marjorie had been making little trips all summer, and for the first two or three days after each arrival home he saw great heaps of mail on the Harveys' hall table addressed to her in various masculine handwritings. To make matters worse, all during the month of August she had been visited by her Cousin Bernice from Eau Claire, and it seemed impossible to see her alone. It was always necessary to hunt round and find someone to take care of Bernice. As August waned this was becoming more and more difficult.

Much as Warren loved Marjorie he had to admit that Cousin Bernice was sorta hopeless. She was pretty, with dark hair and high color, but she was no fun on a party. Every Saturday night he danced a long arduous duty dance with her to please Marjorie, but he had never been anything but bored in her company.

"Warren"—a soft voice at his elbow broke in upon his thoughts, and he turned to see Marjorie, flushed and radiant as usual. She laid a hand on his shoulder and a glow settled almost imperceptibly over him.

"Warren," she whispered "do something for me—dance with Bernice. She's been stuck with little Otis Ormonde for almost an hour."

Warren's glow faded.

"Why—sure," he answered half-heartedly.

"You don't mind, do you? I'll see that you don't get stuck."

"'Sall right."

Marjorie smiled—that smile that was thanks enough.

"You're an angel, and I'm obliged loads."

With a sigh the angel glanced round the veranda, but Bernice and Otis were not in sight. He wandered back inside, and there in front of the women's dressing room he found Otis in the center of a group of young men who were convulsed with laughter. Otis was brandishing a piece of timber he had picked up, and discoursing volubly.

"She's gone in to fix her hair," he announced wildly. "I'm waiting to dance another hour with her."

Their laughter was renewed.

"Why don't some of you cut in?" cried Otis resentfully. "She likes more variety."

"Why, Otis," suggested a friend "you've just barely got used to her."

"Why the two-by-four, Otis?" inquired Warren, smiling.

"The two-by-four? Oh, this? This is a club. When she comes out I'll hit her on the head and knock her in again."

Warren collapsed on a settee and howled with glee.

"Never mind, Otis," he articulated finally. "I'm relieving you this time."

Otis simulated a sudden fainting attack and handed the stick to Warren.

"If you need it, old man," he said hoarsely.

No matter how beautiful or brilliant a girl may be, the reputation of not being frequently cut in on makes her position at a dance unfortunate. Perhaps boys prefer her company to that of the butterflies with whom they dance a dozen times an evening but, youth in this jazz-nourished generation is temperamentally restless, and the idea of fox-trotting more than one full foxtrot with the same girl is distasteful, not to say odious. When it comes to several dances and the intermissions between she can be quite sure that a young man, once relieved, will never tread on her wayward toes again.

Warren danced the next full dance with Bernice, and finally, thankful for the intermission, he led her to a table on the veranda. There was a moment's silence while she did unimpressive things with her fan.

"It's hotter here than in Eau Claire," she said.

Warren stifled a sigh and nodded. It might be for all he knew or cared. He wondered idly whether she was a poor conversationalist because she got no attention or got no attention because she was a poor conversationalist.

"You going to be here much longer?" he asked, and then turned rather red. She might suspect his reasons for asking.

"Another week," she answered, and stared at him as if to lunge at his next remark when it left his lips.

Warren fidgeted. Then with a sudden charitable impulse he decided to try part of his line on her. He turned and looked at her eyes.

"You've got an awfully kissable mouth," he began quietly.

This was a remark that he sometimes made to girls at college proms when they were talking in just such half dark as this. Bernice distinctly jumped. She turned an ungraceful red and became clumsy with her fan. No one had ever made such a remark to her before.

"Fresh!"—the word had slipped out before she realized it, and she bit her lip. Too late she decided to be amused, and offered him a flustered smile.

Warren was annoyed. Though not accustomed to have that remark taken seriously, still it usually provoked a laugh or a paragraph of sentimental banter. And he hated to be called fresh, except in a joking way. His charitable impulse died and he switched the topic.

"Jim Strain and Ethel Demorest sitting out as usual," he commented.

This was more in Bernice's line, but a faint regret mingled with her relief as the subject changed. Men did not talk to her about kissable mouths, but she knew that they talked in some such way to other girls.

"Oh, yes," she said, and laughed. "I hear they've been mooning around for years without a red penny. Isn't it silly?"

Warren's disgust increased. Jim Strain was a close friend of his brother's, and anyway he considered it bad form to sneer at people for not having money. But Bernice had had no intention of sneering. She was merely nervous.

II

When Marjorie and Bernice reached home at half after midnight they said good night at the top of the stairs. Though cousins, they were not intimates. As a matter of fact Marjorie had no female intimates—she considered girls stupid. Bernice on the contrary all through this parent-arranged visit had rather longed to exchange those confidences flavored with giggles and tears that she considered an indispensable factor in all feminine inter-course. But in this respect she found Marjorie rather cold; felt somehow the same difficulty in talking to her that she had in talking to men. Marjorie never giggled, was never frightened, seldom embarrassed, and in fact had very few of the qualities which Bernice considered appropriately and blessedly feminine.

As Bernice busied herself with toothbrush and paste this night she wondered for the hundredth time why she never had any attention when she was away from home. That her family were the wealthiest in Eau Claire; that her mother entertained tremendously, gave little dinners for her daughter before all dances and bought her a car of her own to drive round in, never occurred to her as factors in her home-town social success. Like most girls she had been brought up on the warm milk prepared by Annie Fellows Johnston and on novels in which the female was beloved because of certain mysterious womanly qualities, always mentioned but never displayed.

Bernice felt a vague pain that she was not at present engaged in being popular. She did not know that had it not been for Marjorie's campaigning she would have danced the entire evening with one man; but she knew that even in Eau Claire other girls with less position and less pulchri-tude were given a much bigger rush. She attributed this to something subtly unscrupulous in those girls. It had never worried her, and if it had her mother would have assured her that the other girls cheapened themselves and that men really respected girls like Bernice.

She turned out the light in her bathroom, and on an impulse decided to go in and chat for a moment with her Aunt Josephine, whose light was still on. Her soft slippers bore her noiselessly down the carpeted hall, but hearing voices inside she stopped near the partly opened door. Then she caught her own name, and without any definite intention of eavesdropping lingered—and the thread of the conversation going on inside pierced her consciousness sharply as if it had been drawn through with a needle.

"She's absolutely hopeless!" It was Marjorie's voice. "Oh, I know what you're going to say! So many people have told you how pretty and sweet she is, and how she can cook! What of it? She has a bum time. Men don't like her."

"What's a little cheap popularity?"

Mrs. Harvey sounded annoyed.

"It's everything when you're eighteen," said Marjorie emphatically. "I've done my best. I've been polite and I've made men dance with her, but they just won't stand being bored. When I think of that gorgeous coloring wasted on such a ninny, and think what Martha Carey could do with it—oh!"

"There's no courtesy these days."

Mrs. Harvey's voice implied that modern situations were too much for her. When she was a girl all young ladies who belonged to nice families had glorious times.

"Well," said Marjorie, "no girl can permanently bolster up a lame-duck visitor, because these days it's every girl for herself. I've even tried to drop hints about clothes and things, and she's been furious—given me the funniest looks. She's sensitive enough to know she's not getting away with much, but I'll bet she consoles herself by thinking that she's very virtuous and that I'm too gay and fickle and will come to a bad end. All unpopular girls think that way. Sour grapes! Sarah Hopkins refers to Genevieve and Roberta and me as gardenia girls! I'll bet she'd give ten years of her life and her European education to be a gardenia girl and have three or four men in love with her and be cut in on every few feet at dances."

"It seems to me," interrupted Mrs. Harvey rather wearily, "that you ought to be able to do something for Bernice. I know she's not very vivacious."

Marjorie groaned.

"Vivacious! Good grief! I've never heard her say anything to a boy except that it's hot or the floor's crowded or that she's going to school in New York next year. Sometimes she asks them what kind of car they have and tells them the kind she has. Thrilling!"

There was a short silence and then Mrs. Harvey took up her refrain:

"All I know is that other girls not half so sweet and attractive get partners. Martha Carey, for instance, is stout and loud, and her mother is distinctly common. Roberta

43

Dillon is so thin this year that she looks as though Arizona were the place for her. She's dancing herself to death."

"But, Mother," objected Marjorie impatiently, "Martha is cheerful and awfully witty and an awfully slick girl, and Roberta's a marvelous dancer. She's been popular for ages!"

Mrs. Harvey yawned.

"I think it's that crazy Indian blood in Bernice," continued Marjorie. "Maybe she's a reversion to type. Indian women all just sat round and never said anything."

"Go to bed, you silly child," laughed Mrs. Harvey. "I wouldn't have told you that if I'd thought you were going to remember it. And I think most of your ideas are perfectly idiotic," she finished sleepily.

There was another silence, while Marjorie considered whether or not convincing her mother was worth the trouble. People over forty can seldom be permanently convinced of anything. At eighteen our convictions are hills from which we look; at forty-five they are caves in which we hide.

Having decided this, Marjorie said good night. When she came out into the hall it was quite empty.

III

While Marjorie was breakfasting late next day Bernice came into the room with a rather formal good morning, sat down opposite, stared intently over and slightly moistened her lips.

44

"What's on your mind?" inquired Marjorie, rather puzzled.

Bernice paused before she threw her hand grenade.

"I heard what you said about me to your mother last night."

Marjorie was startled, but she showed only a faintly heightened color and her voice was quite even when she spoke.

"Where were you?"

"In the hall. I didn't mean to listen at first."

After an involuntary look of contempt Marjorie dropped her eyes and became very interested in balancing a stray corn flake on her finger.

"I guess I'd better go back to Eau Claire if I'm such a nuisance." Bernice's lower lip was trembling violently and she continued on a wavering note: "I've tried to be nice, and—and I've been first neglected and then insulted. No one ever visited me and got such treatment."

Marjorie was silent.

"But I'm in the way, I see. I'm a drag on you. Your friends don't like me." She paused, and then remembered another one of her grievances. "Of course I was furious last week when you tried to hint to me that that dress was unbecoming. Don't you think I know how to dress myself?"

"No," murmured less than half aloud.

"What?"

45

"I didn't hint anything," said Marjorie succinctly. "I said, as I remember, that it was better to wear a becoming dress three times straight than to alternate it with two frights."

"Do you think that was a very nice thing to say?"

"I wasn't trying to be nice." Then after a pause: "When do you want to go?"

Bernice drew in her breath sharply.

"Oh!" It was a little half-cry.

Marjorie looked up in surprise.

"Didn't you say you were going?"

"Yes, but—"

"Oh, you were only bluffing!"

They stared at each other across the breakfast table for a moment. Misty waves were passing before Bernice's eyes, while Marjorie's face wore that rather hard expression that she used when slightly intoxicated undergraduates were making love to her.

"So you were bluffing," she repeated as if it were what she might have expected.

Bernice admitted it by bursting into tears. Marjorie's eyes showed boredom.

"You're my cousin," sobbed Bernice. "I'm v-v-visiting you. I was to stay a month, and if I go home my mother will know and she'll wah-wonder—"

Marjorie waited until the shower of broken words collapsed into little sniffles.

"I'll give you my month's allowance," she said coldly, "and you can spend this last week anywhere you want. There's a very nice hotel—"

Bernice's sobs rose to a flute note, and rising of a sudden she fled from the room.

An hour later, while Marjorie was in the library absorbed in composing one of those non-committal, marvelously elusive letters that only a young girl can write, Bernice reappeared, very red-eyed, and consciously calm. She cast no glance at Marjorie but took a book at random from the shelf and sat down as if to read. Marjorie seemed absorbed in her letter and continued writing. When the clock showed noon Bernice closed her book with a snap.

"I suppose I'd better get my ticket."

This was not the beginning of the speech she had rehearsed upstairs, but as Marjorie was not getting her cues—wasn't urging her to be reasonable; it's all a mistake— it was the best opening she could muster.

"Just wait till I finish this letter," said Marjorie without looking round. "I want to get it off in the next mail."

After another minute, during which her pen scratched busily, she turned round and relaxed with an air of "at your service." Again Bernice had to speak.

"Do you want me to go home?"

"Well," said Marjorie, considering, "I suppose if you're not having a good time you'd better go. No use being miserable."

"Don't you think common kindness—"

"Oh, please don't quote!" cried Marjorie impatiently. "That's out of style."

"You think so?"

"Heavens, yes! What modern girl could live like those inane females?"

"They were the models for our mothers."

Marjorie laughed.

"Yes, they were not! Besides, our mothers were all very well in their way, but they know very little about their daughters' problems."

Bernice drew herself up.

"Please don't talk about my mother."

Marjorie laughed.

"I don't think I mentioned her."

Bernice felt that she was being led away from her subject.

"Do you think you've treated me very well?"

"I've done my best. You're rather hard material to work with."

The lids of Bernice's eyes reddened.

"I think you're hard and selfish, and you haven't a feminine quality in you."

"Oh, my Lord!" cried Marjorie in desperation "You little nut! Girls like you are responsible for all the tiresome colorless marriages; all those ghastly inefficiencies that pass as feminine qualities. What a blow it must be when a man with imagination marries the beautiful bundle of clothes

48

that he's been building ideals round, and finds that she's just a weak, whining, cowardly mass of affectations!"

Bernice's mouth had slipped half open.

"The womanly woman!" continued Marjorie. "Her whole early life is occupied in whining criticisms of girls like me who really do have a good time."

Bernice's jaw descended farther as Marjorie's voice rose.

"There's some excuse for an ugly girl whining. If I'd been irretrievably ugly I'd never have forgiven my parents for bringing me into the world. But you're starting life without any handicap—" Marjorie's little fist clinched, "If you expect me to weep with you you'll be disappointed. Go or stay, just as you like." And picking up her letters she left the room.

Bernice claimed a headache and failed to appear at luncheon. They had a matinée date for the afternoon, but the headache persisting, Marjorie made explanation to a not very downcast boy. But when she returned late in the afternoon she found Bernice with a strangely set face waiting for her in her bedroom.

"I've decided," began Bernice without preliminaries, "that maybe you're right about things—possibly not. But if you'll tell me why your friends aren't—aren't interested in me I'll see if I can do what you want me to."

Marjorie was at the mirror shaking down her hair.

"Do you mean it?"

"Yes."

"Without reservations? Will you do exactly what I say?"

"Well, I—"

"Well nothing! Will you do exactly as I say?"

"If they're sensible things."

"They're not! You're no case for sensible things."

"Are you going to make—to recommend—"

"Yes, everything. If I tell you to take boxing lessons you'll have to do it. Write home and tell your mother you're going' to stay another two weeks."

"If you'll tell me—"

"All right—I'll just give you a few examples now. First you have no ease of manner. Why? Because you're never sure about your personal appearance. When a girl feels that she's perfectly groomed and dressed she can forget that part of her. That's charm. The more parts of yourself you can afford to forget the more charm you have."

"Don't I look all right?"

"No; for instance you never take care of your eyebrows. They're black and lustrous, but by leaving them straggly they're a blemish. They'd be beautiful if you'd take care of them in one-tenth the time you take doing nothing. You're going to brush them so that they'll grow straight."

Bernice raised the brows in question.

"Do you mean to say that men notice eyebrows?"

"Yes—subconsciously. And when you go home you ought to have your teeth straightened a little. It's almost imperceptible, still—"

"But I thought," interrupted Bernice in bewilderment, "that you despised little dainty feminine things like that."

"I hate dainty minds," answered Marjorie. "But a girl has to be dainty in person. If she looks like a million dollars she can talk about Russia, ping-pong or the League of Nations and get away with it."

"What else?"

"Oh, I'm just beginning! There's your dancing."

"Don't I dance all right?"

"No, you don't—you lean on a man; yes, you do—ever so slightly. I noticed it when we were dancing together yesterday. And you dance standing up straight instead of bending over a little. Probably some old lady on the side line once told you that you looked so dignified that way. But except with a very small girl it's much harder on the man, and he's the one that counts."

"Go on." Bernice's brain was reeling.

"Well, you've got to learn to be nice to men who are sad birds. You look as if you'd been insulted whenever you're thrown with any except the most popular boys. Why, Bernice, I'm cut in on every few feet—and who does most of it? Why, those very sad birds. No girl can afford to neglect them. They're the big part of any crowd. Young boys too shy to talk are the very best conversational practice. Clumsy boys are the best dancing practice. If you can follow them and yet look graceful you can follow a baby tank across a barb-wire skyscraper."

Bernice sighed profoundly, but Marjorie was not through.

"If you go to a dance and really amuse, say, three sad birds that dance with you; if you talk so well to them that they forget they're stuck with you you've done something. They'll come back next time, and gradually so many sad birds will dance with you that the attractive boys will see there's no danger of being stuck—then they'll dance with you."

"Yes," agreed Bernice faintly. "I think I begin to see."

"And finally," concluded Marjorie, "poise and charm will just come. You'll wake up some morning knowing you've attained it and men will know it too."

Bernice rose.

"It's been awfully kind of you—but nobody's ever talked to me like this before, and I feel sort of startled."

Marjorie made no answer but gazed pensively at her own image in the mirror.

"You're a peach to help me," continued Bernice.

Still Marjorie did not answer, and Bernice thought she had seemed too grateful.

"I know you don't like sentiment," she said timidly.

Marjorie turned to her quickly.

"Oh, I wasn't thinking about that. I was considering whether we hadn't better bob your hair."

Bernice collapsed backward upon the bed.

IV

On the following Wednesday evening there was a dinner-dance at the country club. When the guests strolled in Bernice found her place card with a slight feeling of irritation. Though at her right sat G. Reece Stoddard, a most desirable and distinguished young bachelor, the all-important left held only Charley Paulson. Charley lacked height, beauty, and social shrewdness, and in her new enlightenment Bernice decided that his only qualification to be her partner was that he had never been stuck with her. But this feeling of irritation left with the last of the soup plates, and Marjorie's specific instruction came to her. Swallowing her pride she turned to Charley Paulson and plunged.

"Do you think I ought to bob my hair, Mr. Charley Paulson?"

Charley looked up in surprise.

"Why?"

"Because I'm considering it. It's such a sure and easy way of attracting attention."

Charley smiled pleasantly. He could not know this had been rehearsed. He replied that he didn't know much about bobbed hair. But Bernice was there to tell him.

"I want to be a society vampire, you see," she announced coolly, and went on to inform him that bobbed hair was the necessary prelude. She added that she wanted to ask

53

his advice, because she had heard he was so critical about girls.

Charley, who knew as much about the psychology of women as he did of the mental states of Buddhist contemplatives, felt vaguely flattered.

"So I've decided," she continued, her voice rising slightly, "that early next week I'm going down to the Sevier Hotel barber shop, sit in the first chair, and get my hair bobbed." She faltered, noticing that the people near her had paused in their conversation and were listening; but after a confused second Marjorie's coaching told, and she finished her paragraph to the vicinity at large. "Of course, I'm charging admission, but if you'll all come down and encourage me I'll issue passes for the inside seats."

There was a ripple of appreciative laughter, and under cover of it G. Reece Stoddard leaned over quickly and said close to her ear: "I'll take a box right now."

She met his eyes and smiled as if he had said something surprisingly brilliant.

"Do you believe in bobbed hair?" asked G. Reece in the same undertone.

"I think it's unmoral," affirmed Bernice gravely. "But, of course, you've either got to amuse people or feed 'em or shock 'em." Marjorie had culled this from Oscar Wilde. It was greeted with a ripple of laughter from the men and a series of quick, intent looks from the girls. And then as though she had said nothing of wit or moment

Bernice turned again to Charley and spoke confidentially in his ear.

"I want to ask you your opinion of several people. I imagine you're a wonderful judge of character."

Charley thrilled faintly—paid her a subtle compliment by overturning her water.

Two hours later, while Warren McIntyre was standing passively in the stag line abstractedly watching the dancers and wondering whither and with whom Marjorie had disappeared, an unrelated perception began to creep slowly upon him—a perception that Bernice, cousin to Marjorie, had been cut in on several times in the past five minutes. He closed his eyes, opened them and looked again. Several minutes back she had been dancing with a visiting boy, a matter easily accounted for: a visiting boy would know no better. But now she was dancing with someone else, and there was Charley Paulson headed for her with enthusiastic determination in his eye. Funny—Charley seldom danced with more than three girls an evening.

Warren was distinctly surprised when—the exchange having been effected—the man relieved proved to be none other than G. Reece Stoddard himself. And G. Reece seemed not at all jubilant at being relieved. Next time Bernice danced near, Warren regarded her intently. Yes, she was pretty, distinctly pretty; and tonight her face seemed really vivacious. She had that look that no woman, however histrionically proficient, can successfully counterfeit—she looked as if she were having a good time. He liked the way she had her hair arranged, wondered if it was brilliantine that made it glisten so. And that dress was becoming—a dark red that set off her shadowy eyes and high coloring. He remembered that he had thought her pretty when she first came to town, before he had realized that she was dull. Too bad she was dull—dull girls unbearable—certainly pretty though.

His thoughts zigzagged back to Marjorie. This disappearance would be like other disappearances. When she reappeared he would demand where she had been—would be told emphatically that it was none of his business. What a pity she was so sure of him! She basked in the knowledge that no other girl in town interested him; she defied him to fall in love with Genevieve or Roberta.

Warren sighed. The way to Marjorie's affections was a labyrinth indeed. He looked up. Bernice was again dancing with the visiting boy. Half unconsciously he took a step out from the stag line in her direction, and hesitated. Then he said to himself that it was charity. He walked toward her—collided suddenly with G. Reece Stoddard.

"Pardon me," said Warren.

But G. Reece had not stopped to apologize. He had again cut in on Bernice.

That night at one o'clock Marjorie, with one hand on the electric-light switch in the hall, turned to take a last look at Bernice's sparkling eyes.

"So it worked?"

"Oh, Marjorie, yes!" cried Bernice.

"I saw you were having a gay time."

"I did! The only trouble was that about midnight I ran short of talk. I had to repeat myself—with different men of course. I hope they won't compare notes."

"Men don't," said Marjorie, yawning, "and it wouldn't matter if they did—they'd think you were even trickier."

She snapped out the light, and as they started up the stairs Bernice grasped the banister thankfully. For the first time in her life she had been danced tired.

"You see," said Marjorie at the top of the stairs, "one man sees another man cut in and he thinks there must be something there. Well, we'll fix up some new stuff tomorrow. Good night."

"Good night."

As Bernice took down her hair she passed the evening before her in review. She had followed instructions exactly. Even when Charley Paulson cut in for the eighth time she had simulated delight and had apparently been both interested and flattered. She had not talked about the weather or Eau Claire or automobiles or her school, but had confined her conversation to me, you and us.

But a few minutes before she fell asleep a rebellious thought was churning drowsily in her brain—after all, it was she who had done it. Marjorie, to be sure, had given her her conversation, but then Marjorie got much of her conversation out of things she read. Bernice had bought the red dress, though she had never valued it highly before Marjorie dug it out of her trunk—and her own voice had said the words, her own lips had smiled, her own feet had danced. Marjorie, nice girl—vain, though—nice evening—nice boys—like Warren—Warren—Warren—what's his name—Warren—

She fell asleep.

V

To Bernice the next week was a revelation. With the feeling that people really enjoyed looking at her and listening to her came the foundation of self-confidence. Of course there were numerous mistakes at first. She did not know, for instance, that Draycott Deyo was studying for the ministry; she was unaware that he had cut in on her because he thought she was a quiet, reserved girl. Had she known these things she would not have treated him to the line which began "Hello, Shell Shock!" and continued with the bathtub story—"It takes a frightful lot of energy to fix my hair in the summer—there's so much of it—so I always fix it first and powder my face and put on my hat; then I get into the bathtub, and dress afterward. Don't you think that's the best plan?"

Though Draycott Deyo was in the throes of difficulties concerning baptism by immersion and might possibly have seen a connection, it must be admitted that he did not. He considered feminine bathing an immoral subject, and gave her some of his ideas on the depravity of modern society.

But to offset that unfortunate occurrence Bernice had several signal successes to her credit. Little Otis Ormonde pleaded off from a trip East and elected instead to follow her with a puppylike devotion, to the amusement of his crowd and to the irritation of G. Reece Stoddard, several of whose afternoon calls Otis completely ruined by the disgusting tenderness of the glances he bent on Bernice. He even told her the story of the two-by-four and the dressing room to show her how frightfully mistaken he and everyone else had been in their first judgment of her. Bernice laughed off that incident with a slight sinking sensation.

Of all Bernice's conversation perhaps the best known and most universally approved was the line about the bobbing of her hair.

"Oh, Bernice, when you goin' to get the hair bobbed?"

"Day after tomorrow maybe," she would reply, laughing. "Will you come and see me? Because I'm counting on you, you know."

"Will we? You know! But you better hurry up."

Bernice, whose tonsorial intentions were strictly dishonorable, would laugh again.

"Pretty soon now. You'd be surprised."

But perhaps the most significant symbol of her success was the gray car of the hypercritical Warren McIntyre, parked daily in front of the Harvey house. At first the parlor-maid was distinctly startled when he asked for Bernice instead of Marjorie; after a week of it she told the cook that Miss Bernice had gotta holda Miss Marjorie's best fella.

And Miss Bernice had. Perhaps it began with Warren's desire to rouse jealousy in Marjorie; perhaps it was the familiar though unrecognized strain of Marjorie in Bernice's conversation; perhaps it was both of these and something of sincere attraction besides. But somehow the collective mind of the younger set knew within a week that Marjorie's most reliable beau had made an amazing face-about and was giving an indisputable rush to Marjorie's guest. The question of the moment was how Marjorie would take it. Warren called Bernice on the phone twice a day, sent her notes, and they were frequently seen together in his roadster, obviously engrossed in one of those tense, significant conversations as to whether or not he was sincere.

Marjorie on being twitted only laughed. She said she was mighty glad that Warren had at last found someone who appreciated him. So the younger set laughed, too, and guessed that Marjorie didn't care and let it go at that.

One afternoon when there were only three days left of her visit Bernice was waiting in the hall for Warren, with whom she was going to a bridge party. She was in rather a blissful mood, and when Marjorie—also bound for the party—appeared beside her and began casually to adjust her hat in the mirror, Bernice was utterly unprepared for anything in the nature of a clash. Marjorie did her work very coldly and succinctly in three sentences.

"You may as well get Warren out of your head," she said coldly.

"What?" Bernice was utterly astounded.

"You may as well stop making a fool of yourself over Warren McIntyre. He doesn't care a snap of his fingers about you."

For a tense moment they regarded each other—Marjorie scornful, aloof; Bernice astounded, half angry, half afraid. Then two cars drove up in front of the house and there was a riotous honking. Both of them gasped faintly, turned, and side by side hurried out.

All through the bridge party Bernice strove in vain to master a rising uneasiness. She had offended Marjorie, the sphinx of sphinxes. With the most wholesome and innocent intentions in the world she had stolen Marjorie's property. She felt suddenly and horribly guilty. After the bridge game, when they sat in an informal circle and the conversation became general, the storm gradually broke. Little Otis Ormonde inadvertently precipitated it.

"When you going back to kindergarten, Otis?" someone had asked.

"Me? Day Bernice gets her hair bobbed."

"Then your education's over," said Marjorie quickly. "That's only a bluff of hers. I should think you'd have realized."

"That a fact?" demanded Otis, giving Bernice a reproachful glance.

Bernice's ears burned as she tried to think up an effectual comeback. In the face of this direct attack her imagination was paralyzed.

"There's a lot of bluffs in the world," continued Marjorie quite pleasantly. "I should think you'd be young enough to know that, Otis."

"Well," said Otis, "maybe so. But gee! With a line like Bernice's——"

"Really?" yawned Marjorie. "What's her latest bon mot?"

No one seemed to know. In fact, Bernice, having trifled with her muse's beau, had said nothing memorable of late.

"Was that really all a line?" asked Roberta curiously.

Bernice hesitated. She felt that wit in some form was demanded of her, but under her cousin's suddenly frigid eyes she was completely incapacitated.

"I don't know," she stalled.

"Splush!" said Marjorie. "Admit it!"

Bernice saw that Warren's eyes had left a ukulele he had been tinkering with and were fixed on her questioningly.

"Oh, I don't know!" she repeated steadily. Her cheeks were glowing.

"Splush!" remarked Marjorie again.

"Come through, Bernice," urged Otis. "Tell her where to get off."

Bernice looked round again—she seemed unable to get away from Warren's eyes.

"I like bobbed hair," she said hurriedly, as if he had asked her a question, "and I intend to bob mine."

"When?" demanded Marjorie.

"Any time."

"No time like the present," suggested Roberta.

Otis jumped to his feet.

"Swell stuff!" he cried. "We'll have a summer bobbing party. Sevier Hotel barber shop, I think you said."

In an instant all were on their feet. Bernice's heart throbbed violently.

"What?" she gasped.

Out of the group came Marjorie's voice, very clear and contemptuous.

"Don't worry—she'll back out!"

"Come on, Bernice!" cried Otis, starting toward the door.

Four eyes—Warren's and Marjorie's—stared at her, challenged her, defied her. For another second she wavered wildly.

"All right," she said swiftly "I don't care if I do."

An eternity of minutes later, riding down-town through the late afternoon beside Warren, the others following in Roberta's car close behind, Bernice had all the sensations of Marie Antoinette bound for the guillotine in a tumbrel. Vaguely she wondered why she did not cry out that it was all a mistake. It was all she could do to keep from clutching her hair with both hands to protect it from the suddenly hostile world. Yet she did neither. Even the thought of her mother was no deterrent now. This was the test supreme of her sportsmanship; her right to walk unchallenged in the starry heaven of popular girls.

Warren was moodily silent, and when they came to the hotel he drew up at the curb and nodded to Bernice to precede him out. Roberta's car emptied a laughing crowd into the shop, which presented two bold plate-glass windows to the street.

Bernice stood on the curb and looked at the sign, Sevier Barber Shop. It was a guillotine indeed, and the hangman was the first barber, who, attired in a white coat and smoking a cigarette, leaned nonchalantly against the first chair. He must have heard of her; he must have been waiting all week, smoking eternal cigarettes beside that portentous, too-often-mentioned first chair. Would they blindfold her? No, but they would tie a white cloth round her neck lest any of her blood—nonsense—hair—should get on her clothes.

"All right, Bernice," said Warren quickly.

With her chin in the air she crossed the sidewalk, pushed open the swinging screen door, and giving not a glance to the uproarious, riotous row that occupied the waiting bench, went up to the fat barber.

"I want you to bob my hair."

The first barber's mouth slid somewhat open. His cigarette dropped to the floor.

"Huh?"

"My hair—bob it!"

Refusing further preliminaries, Bernice took her seat on high. A man in the chair next to her turned on his side and gave her a glance, half lather, half amazement. One barber started and spoiled little Willy Schuneman's monthly haircut. Mr. O'Reilly in the last chair grunted and swore musically in ancient Gaelic as a razor bit into his cheek. Two bootblacks became wide-eyed and rushed for her feet. No, Bernice didn't care for a shine.

Outside a passer-by stopped and stared; a couple joined him; half a dozen small boys' noses sprang into life, flattened against the glass; and snatches of conversation borne on the summer breeze drifted in through the screen door.

"Lookada long hair on a kid!"

"Where'd yuh get 'at stuff? 'At's a bearded lady he just finished shavin'."

But Bernice saw nothing, heard nothing. Her only living sense told her that this man in the white coat had removed one tortoise-shell comb and then another; that his fingers were fumbling clumsily with unfamiliar hairpins; that this hair, this wonderful hair of hers, was going—she would never again feel its long voluptuous pull as it hung in a dark-brown glory down her back. For a second she was near breaking down, and then the picture before her swam mechanically into her vision—Marjorie's mouth curling in a faint ironic smile as if to say:

"Give up and get down! You tried to buck me and I called your bluff. You see you haven't got a prayer."

And some last energy rose up in Bernice, for she clinched her hands under the white cloth, and there was a curious narrowing of her eyes that Marjorie remarked on to someone long afterward.

Twenty minutes later the barber swung her round to face the mirror, and she flinched at the full extent of the damage that had been wrought. Her hair was not curls and now it lay in lank lifeless blocks on both sides of her suddenly pale face. It was ugly as sin—she had known it would be ugly as sin. Her face's chief charm had been a Madonna-like simplicity. Now that was gone and she was—well, frightfully mediocre—not stagy; only ridiculous, like a Greenwich Villager who had left her spectacles at home.

As she climbed down from the chair she tried to smile—failed miserably. She saw two of the girls exchange glances; noticed Marjorie's mouth curved in attenuated mockery—and that Warren's eyes were suddenly very cold.

"You see,"—her words fell into an awkward pause—"I've done it."

"Yes, you've—done it," admitted Warren.

"Do you like it?"

There was a half-hearted "Sure" from two or three voices, another awkward pause, and then Marjorie turned swiftly and with serpentlike intensity to Warren.

"Would you mind running me down to Derry's shop?" she asked. "I've simply got to get a hat there before supper. Roberta's driving right home and she can take the others."

Warren stared abstractedly at some infinite speck out the window. Then for an instant his eyes rested coldly on Bernice before they turned to Marjorie.

"Be glad to," he said slowly.

VI

Bernice did not fully realize the outrageous trap that had been set for her until she met her aunt's amazed glance just before dinner.

"Why, Bernice!"

"I've bobbed it, Aunt Josephine."

"Why, child!"

"Do you like it?"

"Why, Ber-nice!"

"I suppose I've shocked you."

"No, but what'll Mrs. Deyo think tomorrow night? Bernice, you should have waited until after the Deyo's dance—you should have waited if you wanted to do that."

"It was sudden, Aunt Josephine. Anyway, why does it matter to Mrs. Deyo particularly?"

"Why, child," cried Mrs. Harvey, "in her paper on The Foibles of the Younger Generation that she read at the last meeting of the Thursday Club she devoted fifteen minutes to bobbed hair. It's her pet abomination. And the dance is for you and Marjorie!"

"I'm sorry."

"Oh, Bernice, what'll your mother say? She'll think I let you do it."

"I'm sorry."

Dinner was an agony. She had made a hasty attempt with a curling iron, and burned her finger and much hair. She could see that her aunt was both worried and grieved, and her uncle kept saying, "Well, I'll be darned!" over and over in a hurt and faintly hostile tone. And Marjorie sat very quietly, intrenched behind a faint smile, a faintly mocking smile.

Somehow she got through the evening. Three boys called; Marjorie disappeared with one of them, and Bernice made a listless unsuccessful attempt to entertain the two others—sighed thankfully as she climbed the stairs to her room at half past ten. What a day!

When she had undressed for the night the door opened and Marjorie came in.

"Bernice," she said "I'm awfully sorry about the Deyo dance. I'll give you my word of honor I'd forgotten all about it."

"'Sall right," said Bernice shortly. Standing before the mirror she passed her comb slowly through her short hair.

"I'll take you down-town tomorrow," continued Marjorie, "and the hairdresser'll fix it so you'll look slick. I didn't imagine you'd go through with it. I'm really mighty sorry."

"Oh, 'sall right!"

"Still it's your last night, so I suppose it won't matter much."

Then Bernice winced as Marjorie tossed her own hair over her shoulders and began to twist it slowly into two long blond braids until in her cream-colored negligée she looked like a delicate painting of some Saxon princess. Fascinated, Bernice watched the braids grow. Heavy and luxurious they were moving under the supple fingers like restive snakes—and to Bernice remained this relic and the curling iron and a tomorrow full of eyes. She could see G. Reece Stoddard, who liked her, assuming his Harvard manner and telling his dinner partner that Bernice shouldn't have been allowed to go to the movies so much; she could see Draycott Deyo exchanging glances with his mother and then being conscientiously charitable to her. But then perhaps by tomorrow Mrs. Deyo would have heard the news; would send round an icy little note requesting that she fail to appear—and behind her back they would all laugh and know that Marjorie had made a fool of her; that her chance at beauty had been sacrificed to the jealous whim of a selfish girl. She sat down suddenly before the mirror, biting the inside of her cheek.

"I like it," she said with an effort. "I think it'll be becoming."

Marjorie smiled.

"It looks all right. For heaven's sake, don't let it worry you!"

"I won't."

"Good night, Bernice."

But as the door closed something snapped within Bernice. She sprang dynamically to her feet, clenching her hands, then swiftly and noiseless crossed over to her bed and from underneath it dragged out her suitcase. Into it she tossed toilet articles and a change of clothing, Then she turned to her trunk and quickly dumped in two drawerfuls of lingerie and summer dresses. She moved quietly, but with deadly efficiency, and in three-quarters of an hour her trunk was locked and strapped and she was fully dressed in a becoming new traveling suit that Marjorie had helped her pick out.

Sitting down at her desk she wrote a short note to Mrs. Harvey, in which she briefly outlined her reasons for going. She sealed it, addressed it, and laid it on her pillow. She glanced at her watch. The train left at one, and she knew that if she walked down to the Marborough Hotel two blocks away she could easily get a taxicab.

Suddenly she drew in her breath sharply and an expression flashed into her eyes that a practiced character reader might have connected vaguely with the set look she had worn in the barber's chair—somehow a development of it. It was quite a new look for Bernice—and it carried consequences.

She went stealthily to the bureau, picked up an article that lay there, and turning out all the lights stood quietly until her eyes became accustomed to the darkness. Softly she pushed open the door to Marjorie's room. She heard the quiet, even breathing of an untroubled conscience asleep.

She was by the bedside now, very deliberate and calm. She acted swiftly. Bending over she found one of the braids of Marjorie's hair, followed it up with her hand to the point nearest the head, and then holding it a little slack so that the sleeper would feel no pull, she reached down with the shears and severed it. With the pigtail in her hand she held her breath. Marjorie had muttered something in her sleep. Bernice deftly amputated the other braid, paused for an instant, and then flitted swiftly and silently back to her own room.

Downstairs she opened the big front door, closed it carefully behind her, and feeling oddly happy and exuberant stepped off the porch into the moonlight, swinging her heavy grip like a shopping bag. After a minute's brisk walk she discovered that her left hand still held the two blond braids. She laughed unexpectedly—had to shut her mouth hard to keep from emitting an absolute peal. She was passing Warren's house now, and on the impulse she set down her baggage, and swinging the braids like piece of rope flung them at the wooden porch, where they landed with a slight thud. She laughed again, no longer restraining herself.

"Huh!" she giggled wildly. "Scalp the selfish thing!"

Then picking up her staircase she set off at a half-run down the moonlit street.

COMMON METER

Rudolph Fisher

Pittsburgh Courier, February 8th 1930

PART I

THE ARCADIA, on Harlem's Lenox Avenue, is "The World's Largest and Finest Ballroom—Admission Eighty-five Cents." Jazz is its holy spirit, which moves it continuously from 9 till 2 every night. Observe above the brilliant entrance this legend in white fire:

TWO—ORCHESTRAS—TWO

Below this in red:

FESS BAXTER'S FIREMEN

Alongside in blue:

BUS WILLIAMS'S BLUE DEVILS

Still lower in gold:

HEAR THEM OUTPLAY EACH OTHER

So much outside. Inside, a blazing lobby, flanked by marble stairways. Upstairs, an enormous dance hall the length of a city block. Low ceilings blushing pink with rows of inverted dome lights. A broad dancing area, bounded on three sides by a wide, soft-carpeted promenade, on the fourth by an ample platform accommodating the two orchestras.

People. Flesh. A fly-thick jam of dancers on the floor, grimly jostling each other; a milling herd of thirsty-eyed boys, moving slowly, searchingly over the carpeted promenade; a congregation of languid girls, lounging in rows of easy-chairs here and there, bodies and faces unconcerned, dark eyes furtively alert. A restless multitude of empty, romance-hungry lives.

Bus Williams's jolly round brown face beamed down on the crowd as he directed his popular hit—"She's Still My Baby."

> You take her out to walk
> And give her baby-talk.
>> But talk or walk, walk or talk—
>> She's still my baby!

But the cheese-colored countenance of Fessenden Baxter, his professional rival, who with his orchestra occupied the adjacent half of the platform, was totally oblivious to "She's Still My Baby."

Baxter had just caught sight of a girl, and catching sight of girls was one of his special accomplishments. Unbelief, wonder, amazement registered in turn on his blunt, bright features. He passed a hand over his straightened brown hair and bent to Perry Parker, his trumpetist.

"P.P. do you see what I see, or is it only the gin?"

"Both of us had the gin," said P.P. "so both of us sees the same thing."

"Judas Priest! Look at that figure, boy!"

"Never was no good at figures," said P.P.

"I've got to get me an armful of that baby."

"Lay off, papa," advised P.P.

"What do you mean, lay off?"

"Lay off. You and your boy got enough to fight over already, ain't you?"

"My boy?"

"Your boy, Bus."

"You mean that's Bus Williams's folks?"

"No lie. Miss Jean Ambrose, lord. The newest hostess. Bus got her the job."

Fess Baxter's eyes followed the girl. "Oh, he got her the job, did he?—Well, I'm going to fix it so she won't need any job. Woman like that's got no business working anywhere."

"Gin," murmured P.P.

"Gin hell," said Baxter. "Gunpowder wouldn't make a mama look as good as that."

"Gunpowder wouldn't make you look so damn good, either."

"You hold the cat's tail," suggested Baxter.

"I'm tryin' to save yours," said P.P.

"Save your breath for that horn."

"Maybe," P.P. insisted, "she ain't so possible as she looks."

"Hush. They can all be taught."

"I've seen some that couldn't."

"Oh you have?—Well, P.P. my boy, remember, that's you."

Beyond the brass rail that limited the rectangular dance area at one lateral extreme, there were many small round tables and clusters of chairs. Bus Williams and the youngest hostess occupied one of these tables while Fess Baxter's Firemen strutted their stuff.

Bus ignored the tall glass before him, apparently endeavoring to drain the girl's beauty with his eyes; a useless effort since it lessened neither her loveliness nor his thirst. Indeed the more he looked the less able was he to stop looking. Oblivious, the girl was engrossed in the crowd. Her amber skin grew clearer and the roses imprisoned in it brighter as her merry black eyes danced over the jostling company.

"Think you'll like it?" he asked.

"Like it?" She was a child of Harlem and she spoke its language. "Boy, I'm having the time of my life. Imagine getting paid for this!"

"You ought to get a bonus for beauty."

"Nice time to think of that—after I'm hired."

"You look like a full course dinner—and I'm starved."

"Hold the personalities, papa."

"No stuff. Wish I could raise a loan on you. Baby—what a roll I'd tote."

"Thanks. Try that big farmer over there hootin' it with Sister Full-bosom. Boy, what a sideshow they'd make!"

"Yea. But what I'm lookin' for is a leadin' lady."

"Yea? I got a picture of any lady leadin' you anywhere."

"You could, Jean."

"Be yourself, brother."

"I ain't bein' nobody else."

"Well, be somebody else, then."

"Remember the orphanage?"

"Time, papa. Stay out of my past."

"Sure—if you let me into your future."

"Speaking of the orphanage—?"

"You wouldn't know it now. They got new buildings all over the place."

"Somehow that fails to thrill me."

"You always were a knockout, even in those days. You had the prettiest hair of any of the girls out there—and the sassiest hip-switch."

"Look at Fred and Adele Astaire over there. How long they been doing blackface?"

"I used to watch you even then. Know what I used to say?"

"Yea. 'Toot-a-toot-toot' on a bugle."

"That ain't all I used to say to myself, 'Boy, when that sister grows up, I'm going to—'."

Her eyes grew suddenly onyx and stopped him like an abruptly reversed traffic signal.

"What's the matter?" he said.

She smiled and began nibbling the straw in her glass.

"What's the matter, Jean?"

"Nothing. Innocence. Nothing. Your boy plays a devilish one-step, doesn't he?"

"Say. You think I'm jivin', don't you?"

"No, darling. I think you're selling insurance."

"Think I'm gettin' previous just because I got you the job."

"Funny, I never have much luck with jobs."

"Well, I don't care what you think. I'm going to say it."

"Let's dance."

"I used to say to myself, 'When that kid grows up, I'm going to ask to marry me."

She called his bluff. "Well, I'm grown up."

"Marry me, will you, Jean?"

Her eyes relented a little in admiration of his audacity. Rarely did a sober aspirant have the courage to mention marriage.

"You're good, Bus. I mean, you're good."

"Every guy ain't a wolf, you know, Jean."

"No. Some are just ordinary meat-hounds."

From the change in his face she saw the depth of the thrust, saw pain where she had anticipated chagrin.

"Let's dance," she suggested again, a little more gently.

They had hardly begun when the number ended, and Fess Baxter stood before them, an ingratiating grin on his Swiss-cheese-colored face.

"Your turn, young fellow," he said to Bus.

"Thoughtful of you, reminding me," said Bus. "This is Mr. Baxter, Miss Ambrose."

"It's always been one of my ambitions," said Baxter, "to dance with a sure-enough angel."

"Just what I'd like to see you doin'," grinned Bus.

"Start up your stuff and watch us," said Baxter. "Step on it, brother. You're holding up traffic."

"Hope you get pinched for speedin'," said Bus, departing.

The Blue Devils were in good form tonight, were really "bearin' down" on their blues. Bus, their leader, however, was only going through the motions, waving his baton idly. His eyes followed Jean and Baxter, and it was nothing to his credit that the jazz maintained its spirit. Occasionally he lost the pair; a brace of young wild birds double-timed through the forest, miraculously avoiding the trees; an extremely ardent couple, welded together, did a decidedly localized mess-around; that gigantic black farmer whom Jean had pointed out sashayed into the line of vision, swung about, backed off, being fancy…

Abruptly, as if someone had caught and held his right arm, Bus's baton halted above his head. His men kept on playing under the impulse of their own momentum, but Bus was a creature apart. Slowly his baton drooped, like the crest of a proud bird, beaten. His eyes died on their object and all his features sagged. On the floor 40 feet away, amid the surrounding clot of dancers, Jean and Baxter had stopped moving and were standing perfectly still. The girl had clasped her partner closer about the shoulders with both arms. Her face was buried in his chest.

Baxter, who was facing the platform, looked up and saw Bus staring. He drew the girl closer, grinning, and shut one eye.

They stood so a moment or an hour till Bus dragged his eyes away. Automatically he resumed beating time. Every moment or so his baton wavered, slowed, and hurried to catch up. The blues were very low-down, the nakedest of jazz, a series of periodic wails against a background of steady, slow rhythm, each pounding pulse descending inevitably, like leaden strokes of fate. Bus found himself singing the words of this grief-stricken lamentation:

> Trouble—trouble has followed me all my days,
> Trouble—trouble has followed my all my days—
> Seems like trouble's gonna follow me always.

The mob demanded an encore, a mob that knew its blues and liked them blue. Bus complied. Each refrain became bluer as it was caught up by a different voice: the wailing clarinet, the weeping C sax, the moaning B flat sax, the trombone, and Bus's own plaintive tenor:

Baby—baby—my baby's gone away,
Baby—baby—my baby's gone away—
Seems like baby—my baby's gone to stay.

Presently the thing beat itself out, and Bus turned to acknowledge applause. He broke a bow off in half. Directly before the platform stood Jean alone, looking up at him.

He jumped down. "Dance?"

"No. Listen. You know what I said at the table?"

"About—wolves?"

"Oh—that—?"

"Yea. I didn't mean anything personal. Honest, I didn't." Her eyes besought his. "You didn't think I meant anything personal, did you?"

"Course not." He laughed. "I know now you didn't mean anything." He laughed again. "Neither one of us meant anything."

Her eyes lifted, widened, fell. "Oh," she said. "Neither one of us meant—anything."

With a wry little smile, he watched her slip off through the crowd.

From his side of the platform Bus overheard Fess Baxter talking to Perry Parker. Baxter had a custom of talking while he conducted, the jazz serving to blanket his words. The blanket was not quite heavy enough tonight.

"P.P., old pooter, she fell."

Parker was resting while the C sax took the lead. "She did?"

"No lie. She says, 'You don't leave me any time for cash customers.'"

"Yea?"

"Yes. And I says, 'I'm a cash customer, baby. Just name your price.'"

Instantly Bus was across the platform and at him, clutched him by the collar, bent him back over the edge of the platform; and it was clear from the look in Bus's eyes that he wasn't just being playful.

"Name her!"

"Hey—what the hell you doin'?"

"Name her or I'll drop you and jump in your face. I swear to—"

"Nellie!" gurgled Fessenden Baxter.

"Nellie who—damn it?"

"Nellie—Gray!"

"All right then!"

Baxter found himself again erect with dizzy suddenness.

The music had stopped, for the players had momentarily lost their breath. Baxter swore and impelled his men into action, surreptitiously adjusting his ruffled plumage.

The crowd had an idea what it was all about and many good-naturedly derided the victim as they passed:

"'Smatter, Fess? Goin' in for toe-dancin'?"

"Nice back-dive, papa, but this ain't no swimmin' pool."

Curry, the large, bald, yellow manager, also had an idea what it was all about and lost no time accosting Bus.

"Tryin' to start somethin'?"

"No. Tryin' to stop somethin'."

"Well, if you gonna stop it with your hands, stop it outside. I ain't got no permit for prize fights in here— 'Course, if you guys can't get on together I can maybe struggle along without one of y' till I find somebody."

Bus said nothing.

"Listen. You birds fight it out with them jazz sticks, y' hear? Them's your weapons. Nex' Monday night's the jazz contest. You'll find out who's the best man next Monday night. Might win more'n a lovin' cup. And y' might lose more. Get me?"

He stood looking sleekly sarcastic a moment, then went to give Baxter like counsel.

Rumor spread through the Arcadia's regulars as night succeeded night.

A pair of buddies retired to the men's room to share a half-pint of gin. One said to the other between gulps:

"Lord today! Ain't them two roosters bearin' down on the jazz!"

"No lie. They mussa had some this same licker."

"Licker hell. Ain't you heard 'bout it?"

"'Bout what?"

"They fightin', Oscar, fightin'."

"Gimme that bottle 'fo' you swaller it. Fightin'? What you mean, fightin'?"

"Fightin' over that new mama."

"The honey-dew?"

"Right. They can't use knives and they can't use knucks. And so they got to fight it out with jazz."

"Yea? Hell of a way to fight."

"That's the only way they'd be any fight. Bus Williams'd knock that yaller boy's can off in a scrap."

"I know it. Y'ought-a seen him grab him las' night."

"I did. They tell me she promised it to the one 'at wins this cup next Monday night."

"Yea? Wisht I knowed some music."

"Sho-nuff sheba all right. I got a long shout with her last night. Papa, she's got everything!"

"Too damn easy on the eyes. Women like that ain't no good 'cep'n to start trouble."

"She sho' could start it for me. I'd 'a' been dancin' with her yet, but my two-bitses give out. Spent two hard-earned bucks dancin' with her, too."

"Shuh! Might as well th'ow yo' money in the street. What you git dancin' with them hostesses?"

"You right there, brother. All I got out o' that one was two dollars worth o' disappointment."

Two girl friends, lounging in adjacent easy-chairs, discussed the situation.

"I can't see what she's got so much more'n anybody else."

"Me neither. I could look a lot better'n that if I didn't have to work all day."

"No lie. Scrubbin' floors never made no bathin' beauties."

"I heard Fess Baxter jivin' her while they was dancin'. He's got a line, no stuff."

"He'd never catch me with it."

"No, dearie. He's got two good eyes too, y'know."

"Maybe that's why he couldn't see you flaggin' 'im."

"Be yourself, sister. He says to her, 'Baby, when the boss hands me that cup.'"

"Hates hisself, don't he?"

"'When the boss hands me that cup,' he says, 'I'm gonna put it right in your arms.'"

"Yea. And I suppose he goes with the cup."

"So she laughs and says, 'Think you can beat him?' So he says, 'Beat him? Huh, that bozo couldn't play a hand-organ.'"

"He don't mean her no good though, this Baxter."

"How do you know?"

"A kack like that never means a woman no good. The other one ast her to step off with him."

"What!"

"Etta Pipp heard him. They was drinkin' and she was at the next table."

"Well, ain't that somethin'! Ast her to step off with him. What'd she say?"

"Etta couldn't hear no more."

"Jus' goes to show ya. What chance has a honest workin' girl got?"

Bus confided in Tappen, his drummer.

"Tap," he said, "ain't it funny how a woman always seems to fall for a wolf?"

"No lie," Tap agreed. "When a guy gets too deep, he's long-gone."

"How do you account for it, Tap?"

"I don't. I jes' play 'em light. When I feel it gettin' heavy—boy, I run like hell."

"Tap, what would you do if you fell for a girl and saw her neckin' another guy?"

"I wouldn't fall," said Tappen, "so I wouldn't have to do nothin'."

"Well, but s'posin' you did?"

"Well, if she was my girl, I'd knock the can off both of 'em."

"S'posin' she wasn't your girl?"

"Well, if she wasn't my girl, it wouldn't be none o' my business."

"Yea, but a guy kind o' hates to see an old friend gettin' jived."

"Stay out, papa. Only way to protect yourself."

"S'posin' you didn't want to protect yourself? S'posin' you wanted to protect the woman?"

"Humph! Who ever heard of a woman needin' protection?"

PART II

"Ladies and gentlemen" sang Curry to the tense crowd that gorged the Arcadia. "Tonight is the night of the only contest of its kind in recorded history! On my left, Mr. Bus Williams, chief of the Blue Devils. On my right, Mr. Fessenden Baxter, leader of the Firemen. On this stand, the solid gold loving cup. The winner will claim the jazz championship of the world!"

"And the sweet mama too, how about it?" called a wag.

"Each outfit will play three numbers: a one-step, a fox-trot, and a blues number. With this stop watch which you see in my hand, I will time your applause after each number. The leader receiving the longest total applause wins the loving cup!"

"Yea—and some lovin'-up wid it!"

"I will now toss a coin to see who plays the first number!"

"Toss it out here!"

"Bus Williams's Blue Devils, ladies and gentlemen, will play the first number!"

Bus's philosophy of jazz held tone to be merely the vehicle of rhythm. He spent much time devising new rhythmic patterns with which to vary his presentations. Accordingly he depended largely on Tappen, his master percussionist, who knew every rhythmic monkey-shine with which to delight a gaping throng.

Bus had conceived the present piece as a chase, in which an agile clarinet eluded impetuous and turbulent traps. The other instruments were to be observers, chorusing their excitement while they urged the principals on.

From the moment the piece started something was obviously wrong. The clarinet was elusive enough, but its agility was without purpose. Nothing pursued it. People stopped dancing in the middle of the number and turned puzzled faces toward the platform. The trap-drummer was going through the motions faithfully but to no avail. His traps were voiceless, emitted mere shadows of sound. He was a deaf mute making a speech.

Brief, perfunctory, disappointed applause rose and fell at the number's end. Curry announced its duration:

"Fifteen seconds flat!"

Fess Baxter, with great gusto, leaped to his post.

"The Firemen will play their first number!"

Bus was consulting Tappen. "For the love o' Pete, Tap—?"

"Love o' hell. Look a' here."

Bus looked—first at the trap-drum, then at the bass; snapped them with a finger, thumped them with his knuckles. There was almost no sound; each drum-sheet was dead, lax instead of taut, and the cause was immediately clear: each bore a short curved knife-cut following its edge a brief distance, a wound unnoticeable at a glance, but fatal to the instrument.

Bus looked at Tappen, Tappen looked at Bus.

"The cream-colored son of a buzzard!"

Fess Baxter, gleeful and oblivious, was directing the crowd about the floor at an exciting, exhausting pace, distorting, expanding, etherealizing their emotions with swift-changing dissonances. Contrary to Bus Williams's philosophy, Baxter considered rhythm a mere rack upon which to hang his tonal tricks. The present piece was dizzy with sudden disharmonies, unexpected twists of phrase, successive false resolutions. Incidentally, however, there was nothing wrong with Baxter's drums.

Boiling over, Bus would have started for him, but Tappen grabbed his coat.

"Hold it, papa. That's a sure way to lose. Maybe we can choke him yet."

"Yea—?"

"I'll play the wood. And I still got cymbals and sandpaper."

"Yea —and a triangle. Hell of a lot o' good they are."

"Can't quit," said Tappen.

"Well," said Bus.

Baxter's number ended in a furor.

"Three minutes and twenty seconds!" bellowed Curry as the applause eventually died out.

Bus began his second number, a foxtrot. In the midst of it he saw Jean dancing, beseeching him with bewildered dismay in her eyes, a look that at once crushed and crazed him. Tappen rapped on the rim of his trap drum, tapped his triangle, stamped the pedal that clapped the cymbals, but the result was a toneless and hollow clatter, a weightless noise that bounced back from the multitude instead of penetrating into it. The players also, distracted by the loss, were operating far below par, and not all their leader's frantic false enthusiasm could compensate for the gaping absence of bass. The very spine had been ripped out of their music, and Tappen's desperate efforts were but the hopeless flutterings of a stricken, limp, pulseless heart.

"Forty-five seconds!" Curry announced. "Making a total so far of one minute flat for the Blue Devils! The Firemen will now play their second number!"

The Firemen's foxtrot was Baxter's rearrangement of Burleigh's "Jean, My Jean," and Baxter, riding his present advantage hard, stressed all that he had put into it of tonal ingenuity. The thing was delirious with strange harmonies, iridescent with odd color changes, and its very flamboyance, its musical fine-writing and conceits delighted the dancers.

But it failed to delight Jean Ambrose, whom by its title it was intended to flatter. She rushed to Bus.

"What is it?" She was a-quiver.

"Drums, gone. Somebody cut the pigskin the last minute."

"What? Somebody? Who?"

"Cut 'em with a knife close to the rim."

"Cut? He cut—? Oh, Bus!" She flashed Baxter a look that would have crumpled his assurance had he seen it. "Can't you— Listen." She was at once wild and calm. "It's the bass. You got to have— I know! Make 'em stamp their feet! Your boys, I mean. That'll do it. All of 'em. Turn the blues into a shout."

"Yea? Gee. Maybe—"

"Try it! You've got to win this thing."

An uproar that seemed endless greeted Baxter's version of "Jean." The girl, back out on the floor, managed to smile as Baxter acknowledged the acclaim by gesturing toward her.

"The present score, ladies and gentlemen, is—for the Blue Devils, one minute even; for the Firemen, six minutes and thirty seconds! The Devils will now play their last number." Curry's intonation of "last" moved the mob to laughter.

Into that laughter Bus grimly led his men like a captain leading his command into fire. He had chosen the parent of blue songs, the old St. Louis Blues, and he adduced every device that had ever adorned that classic. Clarinets wailed, saxophones moaned, trumpets wept wretchedly, trombones laughed bitterly, even the great bass horn sobbed dismally from the depths. And so perfectly did the misery in the music express the actual despair of the situation that the crowd was caught from the start. Soon dancers closed their eyes, forgot their jostling neighbors, lost themselves bodily in the easy sway of that slow, fateful measure, vaguely aware that some quality hitherto lost had at last been found. They were too wholly absorbed to note just how that quality had been found: that every player softly dropped his heel where each bass drum beat would have come, giving each major impulse a body and breadth that no drum could have achieved. Zoom—zoom—zoom—zoom. It was not a mere sound; it was a vibrant throb that took hold of the crowd and rocked it.

They had been rocked thus before, this multitude. Two hundred years ago they had swayed to that same slow fateful measure, lifting their lamentation to heaven, pounding the earth with their feet, seeking the mercy of a new God through the medium of an old rhythm, zoom—zoom. They had rocked so a thousand years ago in a city whose walls were jungle, forfending the wrath of a terrible black God who spoke in storm and pestilence, had swayed and wailed to that same slow period, beaten on a wild boar's skin stretched over the end of a hollow treetrunk. Zoom—zoom—zoom—zoom. Not a sound but an emotion that laid hold on their bodies and swung them into the past. Blues—low-down blues, indeed—blues that reached their souls' depths.

But slowly the color changed. Each player allowed his heel to drop less and less softly. Solo parts faded out, and the orchestra began to gather power as a whole. The rhythm persisted, the unfaltering common meter of blues, but the blueness itself, the sorrow, the despair, began to give way to hope. Ere long hope came to the verge of realization—mounted it—rose above it. The deep and regular impulses now vibrated like nearing thunder, a mighty, inescapable, all-embracing dominance, stressed by the contrast of wind-tones; an all-pervading atmosphere through which soared wild-winged birds. Rapturously, rhapsodically, the number rose to madness and at the height of its madness, burst into sudden silence.

Illusion broke. Dancers awoke, dropped to reality with a jolt. Suddenly the crowd appreciated that Bus Williams had returned to form, had put on a comeback, had struck off a masterpiece. And the crowd showed its appreciation. It applauded its palms sore.

Curry's suspense-ridden announcement ended.

"Total—for the Blue Devils, seven minutes and forty seconds! For the Firemen, six minutes and thirty seconds! Maybe that wasn't the Devils' last number after all. The Firemen will play THEIR last number!"

It was needless for Baxter to attempt the depths and heights just attained by Bus Williams's Blue Devils. His speed, his subordination of rhythm to tone, his exotic coloring, all were useless in a low-down blues song. The crowd moreover had nestled upon the broad, sustaining bosom of a shout. Nothing else warmed them. The end of Baxter's last piece left them chilled and unsatisfied.

But if Baxter realized that he was beaten, his attitude failed to reveal it. Even when the major volume of applause died out in a few seconds, he maintained his self-assured grin. The reason was soon apparent: although the audience as a whole had stopped applauding, two small groups of assiduous hand-clappers, one at either extreme of the dancing area, kept up a diminutive, violent clatter.

Again Bus and Tappen exchanged sardonic stares.

"Damn' if he ain't PAID somebody to clap!"

Only the threatening hisses and boos of the majority terminated this clatter, whereupon Curry summed up:

"For Bus Williams's Blue Devils—seven minutes and forty seconds! For Fess Baxter's Firemen—eight minutes flat!"

He presented Baxter the loving cup amid a hubbub of murmurs, handclaps, shouts, and hisses that drowned out whatever he said. Then the hubbub hushed. Baxter was assisting Jean Ambrose to the platform. With a bow and a flourish he handed the girl the cup.

She held it for a moment in both hands, uncertain, hesitant. But there was nothing uncertain or hesitant in the mob's reaction. Feeble applause was overwhelmed in a deluge of disapprobation. Cries of "Crooked!" "Don't take it!" "Crown the cheat!" "He stole it!" stood out. Tappen put his finger in the slit in his trap-drum, ripped it to a gash, held up the mutilated instrument, and cried, "Look what he done to my traps!" A few hard-boiled ruffians close to the platform moved menacingly toward the victor. "Grab 'im! Knock his can off!"

Jean's uncertainty abruptly vanished. She wheeled with the trophy in close embrace and sailed across the platform toward the defeated Bus Williams. She smiled into his astonished face and thrust the cup into his arms.

"Hot damn, mama! That's the time!" cried a jubilant voice from the floor, and instantly the gathering storm of menace broke into a cloudburst of delight. That romance-hungry multitude saw Bus Williams throw his baton into the air and gather the girl and the loving cup both into his arms. And they went utterly wild—laughed, shouted, yelled and whistled till the walls of the Arcadia bulged.

Jazz emerged as the mad noise subsided: Bus Williams's Blue Devils playing "She's Still My Baby."

In the shelter of a nearby night club Bus and his girl found a secluded corner.

"But you said you didn't mean—anything."

"I'm an awful liar sometimes. Specially when I see my girl giving another guy a play."

"Giving who a play?"

"My boy, Baxter."

"When?"

"Out on the floor that first night. Baby, you draped yourself over him like a Spanish shawl. And there wasn't any movement to speak of."

Her brow cleared and she heaved a sigh. "Well, they say when a guy really falls he quits using his bean."

"He don't go blind, does he?"

"You did. Didn't you see that big farmer step on my foot? For a minute I thought I'd faint!"

SOMETHING FOR NOTHING

John V. Watts

Snappy Stories, June 20th 1926

THE GIRL FROM GEORGIA!

It seems only yesterday that she came into Madame Berthe's seeking employment as a mannikin. I can see Madame now as she put her jeweled hands on her hips and surveyed the girl critically from head to foot, cheap clothes, cheap shoes, and all.

"You want to be a mannikin?" she repeated, as if she couldn't believe her ears.

The girl from Georgia nodded. "Yes, ma'am," she drawled in a husky tone.

"Take off your hat," Madame commanded.

It was the noon hour and the shop was empty of customers. The rest of the girls watched the comedy-drama in the center of the show floor curiously. From the cashier's cage in the balcony I could hear every word that was said.

The girl drew off a faded felt hat and the shaded room seemed to fill with sudden sunlight. Her hair was the most marvelous I had ever seen; a solid, wavy mass of russet gold. Even Madame Berthe, hardened expert in beauty, drew back a pace at its radiance.

"*Mon Dieu*, what hair!" she exclaimed.

"Do you like it?" the girl asked naively. "I'm going to get it bobbed when I get the money."

"Bobbed!" Madame Berthe cried, throwing up her hands in horror. "Bobbed! Idiot!" She turned sharply on the girls clustered around in a circle. "Matilde," she said to one, "take mademoiselle in a room and try that green chiffon on her. Quick!"

It seemed another girl who appeared from the dress room a few moments later. Madame had picked a color that brought out the girl's natural, elusive beauty like dark glass around an ivory cameo.

"But, what a walk!" she wailed when the girl strode around the room. "You come from the country, no?"

"Limona, Georgia, ma'am."

Madame grimaced.

"Well, we do not walk like that in New York. You are not chasing the cows."

Madame waved a hand.

"That is enough," she said. "'You will come in at nine o'clock tomorrow. When," she inquired after a pause, "did you have your last meal?"

The girl from Georgia flushed.

"I had coffee and doughnuts at twelve o'clock."

Madame Berthe signaled to me. "One dollar, Miss Smith," she commanded. "Charge it to Miss— *Sacre*! What is your name, girl?"

"Lucy Bronson, ma'am."

"Br-r-r-r. Do not call me that. It has a 'd' in it. Madame. Madame. Can you say that?"

"Madame," said Lucy Bronson dutifully.

I sent the dollar to Madame in the carrier. The girl took it eagerly, hungrily. She changed quickly, then with a shy glance at the circle of faces around her she was gone, hurrying doubtless to the nearest automat.

I got a clearer conception of the girl from Georgia in the days that followed. She gave an immediate, singularly valid impression of the most dependent, ingenuous type of femininity; she was direct, guileless and astonishingly naive. Her eyes were a striking green, almost translucent, like deep glass held up against a light. She was perfectly formed, her complexion, unmarred by cosmetics, a natural marvel.

Her voice was soft and drawly; in spite of Madame Berthe's coaching she dropped into irresponsible "ma'ams" at every opportunity. She was a constant source of amusement and wonder to the girls, but they treated her kindly, palpably charmed by her innocence.

Toward the end of the week she came to me.

"Miss Smith," she apologized, "I'd like to borrow a little money."

"What do you want with money?" I inquired, assuming my most judicial air.

"I got to pay my rent," she confided. "I'm overdue now. You see, all my money ran out before I got this job. I'll pay you back Saturday if you'll let me have five dollars. Four for the rent and a dollar to eat with tomorrow."

"Where do you live," I asked, "for four dollars a week?"

She mentioned a number on West 49th Street. I wasn't much impressed.

"Listen," I told her, "if you want to live in a decent boarding house, why not come to mine? I'll arrange it with the landlady if you're interested."

That was how the girl from Georgia and I came to live in the same house.

That Sunday night she knocked at my room door.

"I just had to talk to somebody," she said. "I've been to two movies today already."

"Why," I asked, after we had talked of sundry things, "did you come to New York?"

She answered without hesitation.

"To get a rich man."

I must have looked like a fool the way I stared at her. But I couldn't help it. She was dressed in a clean, soft, woolen dress she had evidently bought in the South. It fitted high and close about her slim form, accentuating the curve of her young breast, the simple charm of her slender arms, bare to the elbow. She looked like a schoolgirl, sweet, unsophisticated.

"To get a man!" I repeated.

"Why,'" she asked, looking at me anxiously with her transparent green eyes, "don't you think I can?"

"I thought you were joking," I explained. "What do you want with a rich man?"

She smiled her slow, enveloping smile.

"You wouldn't understand," she said, "unless you'd been raised on a farm—the kind of a farm where I was raised. Silks and satins and pretty shoes and hats and automobiles and a bathtub and lots of nice, fluffy towels like in the magazines. You don't know how you want all those things until you've been raised on a farm."

"Perhaps," I agreed, "but you have to pay a pretty stiff price to get them the way you mean."

"Well," she stated simply, "is there any other way to get them?"

The girl from Georgia, as she soon came to be known at Madame Berthe's, developed rapidly into one of Madame's favorite mannikins. She had an intuition for colors and designs she wore best—and wore them, after little crudities in walk and posture had been ironed out, with a natural charm. Mannerisms of speech and gesture she retained, but they were refreshing in the midst of the cut and dried New York standards.

"Oh, Miss Smith!" she would exclaim during a quiet period in the shop, twisting her lithe young form so that the lines of some lovely gown would show to best advantage. "I'd give half of my life to own this."

Perhaps it was this longing for the beautiful things she wore that enabled her to wear them so well.

Lucy Bronson was too transparent to hold any secrets. The girls knew the second week she was there what had lured her to New York. They kidded her a great deal about it, but she didn't seem to mind.

"Millionaires don't marry," Lucrezia Ganzia, a tall Italian girl told her one day. "They love—but don't marry." There was a bitter undertone in her voice. It was common gossip that some rich young man had spent a pile of money on her once and then dropped her. Lucrezia had been missing from Madame Berthe's for several months. Then she reappeared, seeking work, a changed Lucrezia, hard, cynical, disillusioned.

If Lucy derived any benefit from Lucrezia's remarks she failed to show it. She only shrugged.

It was on a languid day in early summer that Roger Phillips saw Lucy and took a fancy to her. Phillips was about thirty and had inherited several millions from his father, a Long Island real estate operator. He had dropped into Madame Berthe's to pick out an evening wrap for a member of the "Wild Rose" chorus, one of his latest flames.

He saw Lucy and promptly forgot about the wrap she was parading before him.

When Phillips left, Lucy came to me. There was a queer light in her eyes, and her lips were clinched in a firm line.

"Miss Smith," she said, "is that the Roger Phillips you read about in the papers sometimes? The fellow with the money he doesn't know what to do with?"

"That's him," I answered. "And he's certainly a wild one. Why?"

"Nothing," she said, "only he tried to make a date with me for tonight. I didn't, because I wasn't sure he was the Roger Phillips."

My curiosity got the better of me.

"Now," I asked, "what are you going to do?"

"Why, go out with him," she answered complacently.

I made change and then turned to Lucy.

"You'd better leave that young fool alone," I said tartly. "He's a bad egg. He hasn't any more heart than a swordfish. If you read the papers you'll see what he does. A couple of girls have taken poison on account of him; he's been mixed up in some sort of rotten scandal ever since he's been out of short pants."

My words were wasted. Lucy was staring across the balcony into space. For a moment I felt so exasperated that I could have shaken her. But I controlled my anger and, taking up my pencil, went on adding up accounts. When I looked up again she was gone.

Roger Phillips was an early caller at the shop next day. He sought out Lucy Bronson without ado. When he left there was a victorious tilt to his hat that told me plainly that he had made the "date." Lucy told all the girls.

"A millionaire at last," she exclaimed. "What I've been waiting for."

Lucrezia Ganzia sneered.

"If you think you're going to get something for nothing, you're wrong," she said. "Especially from Roger Phillips."

"Don't go out with Phillips," I pleaded, feeling like a motherly aunt. "He's no good. Please, Lucy."

"Miss Smith," she drawled, her eyes filled with tears, "please don't worry about me. I'll be all right. I can take care of myself. It's too good a chance to miss. I might never have another. Please don't worry about me."

I couldn't budge her. But, persistence being one of my few outstanding traits, I continued to watch over her secretly. Her room was next to mine. I would sit up late reading until she came in, then I would go to bed, hoping for the best. She went out with Phillips constantly. She showed me gifts she got from him; a platinum wrist watch, a small chain of pearls, a bracelet, a wrap. And I knew from the steadiness of her gaze when she spoke of him that she was still the unsophisticated Lucy.

The crisis came, as crises do, unexpectedly. It was the Saturday night of the third week of Lucy's acquaintance with Roger Phillips, and I had gone to a movie. After the show, alone in my room, I sat up reading a book, listening subconsciously for Lucy to come in. At midnight she had not returned; at one, alarmed, I opened the door of her room. It was empty; she had not been home.

Throwing on a cloak I ran down the stairs to the telephone book. Phillips, I knew, lived in an apartment somewhere on Park Avenue, but I did not know the number. I thumbed the big directory feverishly. Finally I found it.

As I ran to Broadway to catch a taxi I blamed myself over and over for what had happened.

"You should have spanked her good and hard," I repeated as the taxi turned into Park Avenue. "Locked her in her room; anything to have saved her from this. The poor little babe in the woods."

The taxi stopped with a squeak before a huge apartment house. Bidding the driver wait, I ran into the lobby. There a combination elevator and telephone boy stopped me.

"'I want to go up to Roger Phillips's apartment," I told him.

He eyed me suspiciously.

"Who do?" he wanted to know.

I could have killed him without the least compunction.

"Oh, he doesn't know me. But I must see him—it's important. I must see him."

The negro continued to bar my way.

"Can't see nobody," he declared, "unless you know 'em. It's agin the rules. You kin phone if you wanta."

I swallowed my anger. What could I do telephoning? But I had the boy ring the apartment. There was a long silence, then a man's voice.

"Is Lucy Bronson there?" I demanded.

Another pause.

"No," the voice said. It was Phillips, I knew. And I knew also intuitively that he had lied. But before I could say anything more the receiver was hung up in my ear.

Defeated, I walked out of the lobby. Goodness knows, I had tried. It was her own fault, the little idiot. I had done everything I could. But a stronger inner voice drowned out these arguments. The memory of Lucy Bronson, fresh, pure, trusting, rose before me.

I would have to use strategy, I decided. Paying the taxi driver I walked down the avenue. A few minutes later I was back, keeping myself hidden from the elevator boy and watching for a chance to sneak into the lobby and up the stairs.

Finally my opportunity came. A taxi pulled up and a couple alighted. They got into the elevator with the negro and disappeared upward.

Quickly I sneaked into the lobby, feeling like a thief, and ran up the stairs. On the third floor I found Phillips's apartment. I tried the door gently. It was locked, of course. For a moment I debated whether or not to knock, deciding against it. If Phillips answered he would probably slam the door in my face.

I paced the hall, revolving a hundred plans in my brain. And at length, as I noticed that the apartment was at the end of the hall, I resolved to climb out on the fire escape, try to catch sight of Lucy through the window, and then call the police.

Gingerly I let myself on the fire escape and crouched, peering into the apartment.

If the world had suddenly come to an end I could not have been more surprised at what I saw. Lucy Bronson, her bright golden hair in disarray, was sitting rakishly on a divan, part of a cocktail at her elbow. Beside her, swaying unsteadily, was Roger Phillips. He had just finished a drink. A teacart was drawn up beside them, loaded with cigarettes, glasses and bottles.

Petrified with amazement, I stared. Could this be Lucy Bronson, the simple girl of the country? I rubbed my eyes and stared again. Yes, it was she; there was no mistake. And, even as I looked, Phillips sat down beside her and kissed her. I can see Lucy now as she put her red lips to be kissed.

Sickened and weak, I crept back into the hall, and down through the empty lobby to the street. The fresh air revived me a little. Somehow I got another taxi and went back to my room.

The papers the next day were full of the news. How a modiste's model had married Roger Phillips and his millions; how a simple girl from Limona, Georgia, had bewitched one of the season's most sought-after bachelors; Cinderella and the Prince all over again, details of the Phillips fortune, Phillips's clubs, reported engagements, the divorce from his first wife, so forth and so forth. One of the papers had a photograph of Lucy.

She came into Madame Berthe's a few months ago, the girl from Georgia, to order a lot of new gowns and cloaks. She had just won a separation decree from Roger Phillips with $50,000 a year alimony. She stopped at my desk for a moment and looked at me with her translucent eyes.

"It was funny, Miss Smith," she said gravely, "but I wasn't really sure of landing Roger until you mentioned that he would try to get me to drink too much as he did other girls. That gave me an idea immediately. All I would have to do would be to get *him* tipsy instead. A man who's plastered will do anything, even marry."

"But," I replied, a light beginning to dawn on me, "weren't you afraid of his getting you there first?"

The girl from Georgia shook her head.

"No," she said, "you see, dad ran the biggest still in the county till he got bumped off."

THE MANTLE OF WHISTLER

Dorothy Parker

New Yorker, August 18th 1928

T HE HOSTESS, all smiles and sparkles and small, abortive dance steps, led the young man with the sideburns across the room to where sat the girl who had twice been told she looked like Clara Bow.

"There she is!" she cried. "Here's the girl we've been looking for! Miss French, let me make you acquainted with Mr. Bartlett."

"Pleased to meet up with you social," said Mr. Bartlett.

"Pardon my wet glove," said Miss French.

"Oh, you two!" said the hostess. "I've just been dying to get you two together. I knew you'd get on just like nothing at all. Didn't I tell you he had a marvelous line, Alice? What'd I tell you, Jack—didn't I say over and over again she was a scream? And she's always like this. You wait till you know her as well as I do! Goodness, I just wish I could stay here and listen to you."

However, frustrated in her desire, she smiled heartily, waved her hand like a dear little baby shaking bye-bye, and schottisched across the floor to resume the burdens of hospitality.

"Hey, where have you been all my life?" said the young man who had a marvelous line.

"Don't be an Airedale," said the girl who was always like this.

"Any objection if I sit down?" he said.

"Go right ahead," she said. "Sit down and take a load off your feet."

"I'll do that little thing for you," he said. "Sit down before I fall down, what? Some party, isn't it? What a party this turned out to be!"

"And how!" she said.

"'And how' is right," he said. "'S wonderful."

"'S marvelous," she said.

"'S awful nice," he said.

"'S Paradise," she said.

"Right there with the comeback, aren't you?" he said. "What a girl you turned out to be! Some girl, aren't you?"

"Oh, don't be an Airedale," she said.

"Just a real good girl," he said. "Some little looker, too. Where did you get those big, blue eyes from, anyway? Don't you know I'm the guy that always falls for big, blue eyes?"

"You would," she said. "You're just the tripe."

"Hey, listen, listen," he said. "Lay off for a minute, will you? Come on, now, get regular. Aren't you going to tell me where you got those big, blue eyes?"

"Oh, don't be ridic," she said. "They are not big! Are they?"

"Are they big!" he said. "You don't know they're big, do you? Oh, no, nobody ever told you that before. And you don't know what you do to me, when you look up like that, do you? Yes, you don't!"

"I wouldn't know about that," she said.

"Ah, stop that, will you?" he said. "Go ahead, now, come clean. Tell me where you got those big, blue eyes."

"What's your idea in bringing that up?" she said.

"And your hair's pretty cute, too," he said. "I suppose you don't know you've got pretty cute hair. You wouldn't know about that, would you?"

"Even if that was good, I wouldn't like it," she said.

"Come on, now, Miss Moran and Mack," he said. "Don't you know that hair of yours is pretty cute?"

"'S wonderful," she said. "'S marvelous."

"That you should care for me?" he said.

"Oh, don't be an Airedale," she said.

"I could care for you in a big way," he said. "What those big, blue eyes of yours do to me is nobody's business. Know that?"

"Oh, I wouldn't know about that," she said.

"Hey, listen," he said, "what are you trying to do—run me ragged? Don't you ever stop kidding? When are you going to tell me where you got your big, blue eyes?"

"Oh, pull yourself together," she said.

"I'd have to have a care with a girl like you," he said. "Watch my step, that's what I'd have to do."

"Don't be sil," she said.

"You know what?" he said. "I could get a girl like you on the brain."

"The what?" she said.

"Ah, come on, come on," he said. "Lay off that stuff, will you? Tell me where you've been keeping yourself, anyhow. Got any more like you around the house?"

"'S all there is," she said. "'R' isn't any more."

"That's K.O. with me," he said. "One like you's enough. What those eyes of yours do to me is plenty! Know it?"

"I wouldn't know about that," she said.

"That dress of yours slays me," he said. "Where'd you get the catsy dress? Hm?"

"Don't be an Airedale," she said.

"Hey, where'd you get that expression, anyway?" he said.

"It's a gift," she said.

"'Gift' is right," he said. "And how."

"You ain't heard nothin' yet," she said.

"You slay me," he said. "I'm telling you. Where do you get all your stuff from?"

"What's your idea in bringing that up?" she said.

*

The hostess, with enhanced sparkles, romped over to them.

"Well, for heaven's sakes!" she cried. "Aren't you two even going to look at anybody else? What do you think of her, Jack? Isn't she cute?"

"Is she cute!" he said.

"Isn't he marvelous, Alice?" asked the hostess.

"You'd be surprised," she said.

The hostess cocked her head, like a darling, mischievous terrier puppy, and sparkled whimsically at them.

"Oh, you two!" she said. "Didn't I tell you you'd get on just like nothing at all?"

"And how!" said the girl who was always like this.

"'And how' is right!" said the young man who had the marvelous line.

"You two!" cooed the hostess. "I could listen to you all night."

NIGHT CLUB

Katharine Brush

Harper's Magazine, September 1927

P ROMPTLY at quarter of 10 p.m. Mrs. Brady descended the steps of the Elevated. She purchased from the newsdealer in the cubbyhole beneath them a next month's magazine and a tomorrow morning's paper and, with these tucked under one plump arm, she walked. She walked two blocks north on Sixth Avenue; turned and went west. But not far west. Westward half a block only, to the place where the gay green awning marked Club Français paints a stripe of shade across the glimmering sidewalk. Under this awning Mrs. Brady halted briefly, to remark to the six-foot doorman that it looked like rain and to await his performance of his professional duty. When the small green door yawned open, she sighed deeply and plodded in.

The foyer was a blackness, an airless velvet blackness like the inside of a jeweler's box. Four drum-shaped lamps of golden silk suspended from the ceiling gave it light (a very little) and formed the jewels: gold signets, those, or cufflinks for a giant. At the far end of the foyer there were black stairs, faintly dusty, rippling upward toward an amber radiance. Mrs. Brady approached and ponderously mounted the stairs, clinging with one fist to the mangy velvet rope that railed their edge.

From the top, Miss Lena Levin observed the ascent. Miss Levin was the checkroom girl. She had dark-at-the-roots blond hair and slender hips upon which, in moments of leisure, she wore her hands, like buckles of ivory loosely attached. This was a moment of leisure. Miss Levin waited behind her counter. Row upon row of hooks, empty as yet, and seeming to beckon—wee curved fingers of iron— waited behind her.

"Late," said Miss Levin, "again."

"Go wan!" said Mrs. Brady. "It's only ten to ten. *Whew!* Them *stairs!*"

She leaned heavily, sideways, against Miss Levin's counter, and, applying one palm to the region of her heart, appeared at once to listen and to count. "Feel!" she cried then in a pleased voice.

Miss Levin obediently felt.

"Them stairs," continued Mrs. Brady darkly, "with my bad heart, will be the death of me. Whew! Well, dearie? What's the news?"

"You got a paper," Miss Levin languidly reminded her.

"Yeah!" agreed Mrs. Brady with sudden vehemence. "I got a paper!" She slapped it upon the counter. "An' a lot of time I'll get to *read* my paper, won't I now? On a Saturday night!" She moaned. "Other nights is bad enough, dear knows—but *Saturday* nights! How I dread 'em! Every Saturday night I say to my daughter, I say, 'Geraldine, I can't,' I say, 'I can't go through it again, an' that's all there is to it,' I say. 'I'll *quit!*' I say. An' I *will*, too!" added Mrs. Brady firmly, if indefinitely.

Miss Levin, in defense of Saturday nights, mumbled some vague something about tips.

"Tips!" Mrs. Brady hissed it. She almost spat it. Plainly money was nothing, nothing at all, to this lady. "I just wish," said Mrs. Brady, and glared at Miss Levin, "I just wish *you* had to spend one Saturday night, just one, in that dressing room! Bein' pushed an' stepped on and near knocked down by that gang of hussies, an' them orderin' an' bossin' you 'round like you was *black*, an' usin' your things an' then sayin' they're sorry, they got no change, they'll be back. Yah! They *never* come back!"

"There's Mr. Costello," whispered Miss Levin through lips that, like a ventriloquist's, scarcely stirred.

"An' as I was sayin'," Mrs. Brady said at once brightly, "I got to leave you. Ten to ten, time I was on the job."

She smirked at Miss Levin, nodded, and right-about-faced. There, indeed, Mr. Costello was. Mr. Billy Costello, manager, proprietor, monarch of all he surveyed. From the doorway of the big room, where the little tables herded in a ring around the waxen floor, he surveyed Mrs. Brady, and in such a way that Mrs. Brady, momentarily forgetting her bad heart, walked fast, scurried faster, almost ran.

The door of her domain was set politely in an alcove, beyond silken curtains looped up at the sides. Mrs. Brady reached it breathless, shouldered it open; and groped for the electric switch. Lights sprang up, a bright white blaze, intolerable for an instant to the eyes, like sun on snow. Blinking, Mrs. Brady shut the door.

The room was a spotless, white-tiled place, half beauty shop, half dressing room. Along one wall stood washstands, sturdy triplets in a row, with pale-green liquid soap in glass balloons afloat above them. Against the opposite wall there was a couch. A third wall backed an elongated glass-topped dressing table; and over the dressing table and over the washstands long rectangular sheets of mirror reflected lights, doors, glossy tiles, lights multiplied…

Mrs. Brady moved across this glitter like a thick dark cloud in a hurry. At the dressing table she came to a halt, and upon it she laid her newspaper, her magazine, and her purse—a black purse worn gray with much clutching. She divested herself of a rusty black coat and a hat of the mushroom persuasion, and hung both up in a corner cupboard which she opened by means of one of a quite preposterous bunch of keys. From a nook in the cupboard she took down a lace edged handkerchief with long streamers. She untied the streamers and tied them again around her chunky black alpaca waist. The handkerchief became an apron's baby cousin.

Mrs. Brady relocked the cupboard door, fumbled her key-ring over, and unlocked a capacious drawer of the dressing table. She spread a fresh towel on the plate-glass top, in the geometrical center, and upon the towel she arranged with care a procession of things fished from the drawer. Things for the hair. Things for the complexion. Things for the eyes, the lashes, the brows, the lips, and the fingernails. Things in boxes and things in jars and things in tubes and tins. Also, an ashtray, matches, pins, a tiny sewing kit, a pair of scissors. Last of all, a hand-printed sign, a nudging sort of sign:

NOTICE!

These Articles, Placed Here For Your Convenience,
Are The Property Of The *Maid*.

And directly beneath the sign, propping it up against the looking-glass, a china saucer, in which Mrs. Brady now slyly laid decoy money: two quarters and two dimes, in four-leaf-clover formation.

Another drawer of the dressing table yielded a bottle of bromo-seltzer, a bottle of aromatic spirits of ammonia, a tin of sodium bicarbonate, and a teaspoon. These were lined up on a shelf above the couch.

Mrs. Brady was now ready for anything. And (from the grim, thin pucker of her mouth) expecting it.

Music came to her ears. Rather, the beat of music, muffled, rhythmic, remote. *Umpa-um, umpa-um, umpa-um-mm*—Mr. "Fiddle" Baer and his band, hard at work on the first foxtrot of the night. It was teasing, foot-tapping music; but the large solemn feet of Mrs. Brady were still. She sat on the couch and opened her newspaper; and for some moments she read uninterruptedly, with special attention to the murders, the divorces, the breaches of promise, the funnies.

Then the door swung inward, admitting a blast of Mr. "Fiddle" Baer's best, a whiff of perfume, and a girl.

Mrs. Brady put her paper away.

The girl was *petite* and darkly beautiful; wrapped in fur and mounted on tall jeweled heels. She entered humming the ragtime song the orchestra was playing, and while she stood near the dressing table, stripping off her gloves, she continued to hum it softly to herself:

Oh, I know my baby loves me,
I can tell my baby loves me.

Here the dark little girl got the left glove off, and Mrs. Brady glimpsed a platinum wedding ring.

'Cause there ain't no maybe
In my baby's
Eyes.

The right glove came off. The dark little girl sat down in one of the chairs that faced the dressing table. She doffed her wrap, casting it carelessly over the chair back. It had a cloth-of-gold lining, and "Paris" was embroidered in curlicues on the label. Mrs. Brady hovered solicitously near.

The dark little girl, still humming; looked over the articles "placed here for your convenience," and picked up the scissors. Having cut off a very small hangnail with the air of one performing a perilous major operation, she seized and used the manicure buffer, and after that the eyebrow pencil. Mrs. Brady's mind, hopefully calculating the tip, jumped and jumped again like a taxi meter.

Oh, I know my baby loves me—

The dark little girl applied powder and lipstick belonging to herself. She examined the result searchingly in the mirror and sat back, satisfied. She cast some silver *Klink! Klink!* into Mrs. Brady's saucer, and half rose. Then, remembering something, she settled down again.

The ensuing thirty seconds were spent by her in pulling off her platinum wedding ring, tying it in a corner of a lace handkerchief, and tucking the handkerchief down the bodice of her tight white-velvet gown.

"There!" she said.

She swooped up her wrap and trotted toward the door, jeweled heels merrily twinkling.

'Cause there ain't no maybe—

The door fell shut.

Almost instantly it opened again, and another girl came in. A blond, this. She was pretty in a round-eyed, babyish way; but Mrs. Brady, regarding her, mentally grabbed the spirits of ammonia bottle. For she looked terribly ill. The round eyes were dull, the pretty, silly little face was drawn. The thin hands, picking at the fastenings of a specious beaded bag, trembled and twitched.

Mrs. Brady cleared her throat. "Can I do something for you, Miss?"

Evidently the blond girl had believed herself alone in the dressing room. She started violently, and glanced up, panic in her eyes. Panic, and something else. Something very like murderous hate—but for an instant only, so that Mrs. Brady, whose perceptions were never quick, missed it altogether.

"A glass of water?" suggested Mrs. Brady.

"No," said the girl, "no." She had one hand in the beaded bag now. Mrs. Brady could see it moving, causing the bag to squirm like a live thing, and the fringe to shiver. "Yes!" she cried abruptly. "A glass of water—please—you get it for me."

She dropped onto the couch. Mrs. Brady scurried to the water cooler in the corner, pressed the spigot with a determined thumb. Water trickled out thinly. Mrs. Brady pressed harder, and scowled, and thought, "Something's

122

wrong with this thing. I mustn't forget, next time I see Mr. Costello—"

When again she faced her patient, the patient was sitting erect. She was thrusting her clenched hand back into the beaded bag again.

She took only a sip of the water, but it seemed to help her quite miraculously. Almost at once color came to her cheeks, life to her eyes. She grew young again—as young as she was. She smiled up at Mrs. Brady.

"Well!" she exclaimed. "What do you know about that!" She shook her honey-colored head. "I can't imagine what came over me."

"Are you better now?" inquired Mrs. Brady.

"Yes. Oh, yes. I'm better now. You see," said the blond girl confidentially, "we were at the theater, my boyfriend and I, and it was hot and stuffy—I guess that must have been the trouble." She paused, and the ghost of her recent distress crossed her face. "God! I thought that last act *never* would end!" she said.

While she attended to her hair and complexion, she chattered gayly to Mrs. Brady, chattered on with scarcely a stop for breath, and laughed much. She said, among other things, that she and her "boyfriend" had not known one another very long, but that she was "ga-ga" about him. "He is about me, too," she confessed. "He thinks I'm grand."

She fell silent then, and in the looking-glass her eyes were shadowed, haunted. But Mrs. Brady, from where she stood, could not see the looking-glass; and half a minute later the blond girl laughed and began again. When she went out she seemed to dance out on little winged feet; and Mrs. Brady, sighing, thought it must be nice to be young... and happy like that.

The next arrivals were two. A tall, extremely smart young woman in black chiffon entered first, and held the door open for her companion; and the instant the door was shut, she said, as though it had been on the tip of her tongue for hours, "Amy, what under the sun *happened*?"

Amy, who was brown-eyed, brown-bobbed-haired, and patently annoyed about something, crossed to the dressing table and flopped into a chair before she made reply.

"Nothing," she said wearily then.

"That's nonsense!" snorted the other. "Tell me. Was it something she said? She's a tactless ass, of course. Always was."

"No, not anything she said. It was—" Amy bit her lip. "All right! I'll tell you. Before we left your apartment I just happened to notice that Tom had disappeared. So I went to look for him—I wanted to ask him if he'd remembered to tell the maid where we were going—Skippy's subject to croup, you know, and we always leave word. Well, so I went into the kitchen, thinking Tom might be there mixing cocktails—and there he was—and there *she* was!"

The full red mouth of the other young woman pursed itself slightly. Her arched brows lifted. "Well?"

Her matter-of-factness appeared to infuriate Amy. "He was *kissing* her!" she flung out.

"Well?" said the other again. She chuckled softly and patted Amy's shoulder, as if it were the shoulder of a child. "You're surely not going to let *that* spoil your whole evening? Amy *dear*! Kissing may once have been serious and significant—but it isn't nowadays. Nowadays, it's like shaking hands. It means nothing."

But Amy was not consoled. "I hate her!" she cried desperately. "Red-headed *thing*! Calling me 'darling' and 'honey,' and s-sending me handkerchiefs for C-Christmas—and then sneaking off behind closed doors and k-kissing my h-h-husband…"

At this point Amy quite broke down, but she recovered herself sufficiently to add with venom, "I'd like to slap her!"

"Oh, oh, oh," smiled the tall young woman, "I wouldn't do that!"

Amy wiped her eyes with what might well have been one of the Christmas handkerchiefs, and confronted her friend. "Well, what *would* you do, Claire ? If you were I?"

"I'd forget it," said Claire, "and have a good time. I'd kiss somebody myself. You've no idea how much better you'd feel!"

"I don't do—" Amy began indignantly; but as the door behind her opened and a third young woman—red-headed, earringed, exquisite—lilted in, she changed her tone. "Oh, hello!" she called sweetly, beaming at the newcomer via the mirror. "We were wondering what had become of you!"

The red-headed girl, smiling easily back, dropped her cigarette on the floor and crushed it out with a silver-shod toe. "Tom and I were talking to 'Fiddle' Baer," she explained. "He's going to play 'Clap Yo' Hands' next, because it's my favorite. Lend me a comb, will you, somebody?"

"There's a comb there," said Claire, indicating Mrs. Brady's business comb.

"But imagine using it!" murmured the red-headed girl. "Amy, darling, haven't you one?"

Amy produced a tiny comb from her rhinestone purse. "Don't forget to bring it when you come," she said, and stood up. "I'm going on out, I want to tell Tom something."

She went.

The red-headed young woman and the tall black-chiffon one were alone, except for Mrs. Brady. The red-headed one beaded her incredible lashes. The tall one, the one called Claire, sat watching her. Presently she said, "Sylvia, look here." And Sylvia looked. Anybody, addressed in that tone, would have.

"There is one thing," Claire went on quietly, holding the other's eyes, "that I want understood. And that is, *'Hands off!'* Do you hear me?"

"I don't know what you mean."

"You do know what I mean!"

The red-headed girl shrugged her shoulders. "Amy told you she saw us, I suppose."

"Precisely. And," went on Claire, gathering up her possessions and rising, "as I said before, you're to keep away." Her eyes blazed sudden white-hot rage. "Because, as you very well know, he belongs to *me*," she said, and departed, slamming the door.

Between eleven o'clock and one Mrs. Brady was very busy indeed. Never for more than a moment during those two hours was the dressing room empty. Often it was jammed, full to overflowing with curled cropped heads, with ivory arms and shoulders, with silk and lace and chiffon, with legs. The door flapped in and back, in and back. The mirrors caught and held—and lost—a hundred different faces. Powder veiled the dressing table with a thin white dust; cigarette stubs, scarlet at the tips, choked the ash-receiver. Dimes and quarters clattered into Mrs. Brady's saucer—and were transferred to Mrs. Brady's purse. The original seventy cents remained. That much, and no more, would Mrs. Brady gamble on the integrity of womankind.

She earned her money. She threaded needles and took stitches. She powdered the backs of necks. She supplied towels for soapy, dripping hands. She removed a speck from a teary blue eye and pounded the heel on a slipper. She curled the straggling ends of a black bob and a gray bob, pinned a velvet flower on a lithe round waist, mixed three doses of bicarbonate of soda, took charge of a shed pink-satin girdle, collected, on hands and knees, several dozen fake pearls that had wept from a broken string.

She served chorus girls and school girls, gay young matrons and gayer young mistresses, a lady who had divorced four husbands, and a lady who had poisoned one, the secret (more or less) sweetheart of a Most Distinguished Name, and the Brains of a bootleg gang… She saw things. She saw a yellow check, with the ink hardly dry. She saw four tiny bruises, such as fingers might make, on an arm. She saw a girl strike another girl, not playfully. She saw a bundle of letters some man wished he had not written, safe and deep in a brocaded handbag.

About midnight the door flew open and at once was pushed shut, and a gray-eyed, lovely child stood backed against it, her palms flattened on the panels at her sides, the draperies of her white chiffon gown settling lightly to rest around her.

There were already five damsels of varying ages in the dressing room. The latest arrival marked their presence with a flick of her eyes and, standing just where she was, she called peremptorily, "Maid!"

Mrs. Brady, standing just where she was, said, "Yes, miss?"

"Please come here," said the girl.

Mrs. Brady, as slowly as she dared, did so.

The girl lowered her voice to a tense half-whisper. "Listen! Is there a way I can get out of here except through this door I came in?"

Mrs. Brady stared at her stupidly.

"Any window?" persisted the girl. "Or anything?"

Here they were interrupted by the exodus of two of the damsels-of-varying-ages. Mrs. Brady opened the door for them—and in so doing caught a glimpse of a man who waited in the hall outside, a debonair, old-young man with a girl's furry wrap hung over his arm, and his hat in his hand.

The door clicked. The gray-eyed girl moved out from the wall, against which she had flattened herself—for all the world like one eluding pursuit in a cinema.

"What about that window?" she demanded, pointing.

"That's all the farther it opens," said Mrs. Brady.

"Oh! And it's the only one—isn't it?"

"It is."

"Damn," said the girl. "Then there's *no* way out?"

"No way but the door," said Mrs. Brady testily.

The girl looked at the door. She seemed to look *through* the door, and to despise and to fear what she saw. Then she looked at Mrs. Brady. "Well," she said, "then I s'pose the only thing for me to do is to stay in here."

She stayed. Minutes ticked by. Jazz crooned distantly, stopped, struck up again. Other girls came and went. Still the gray-eyed girl sat on the couch, with her back to the wall and her shapely legs crossed, smoking cigarettes, one from the stub of another.

After a long while she said, "Maid!"

"Yes, miss?"

"Peek out that door, will you, and see if there's anyone standing there."

Mrs. Brady peeked, and reported that there was. There was a gentleman with a little bit of a black mustache standing there. The same gentleman, in fact, who was standing there "just after you come in."

"Oh, Lord," sighed the gray-eyed girl. "Well… I can't stay here all *night*, that's one sure thing."

She slid off the couch, and went listlessly to the dressing table. There she occupied herself for a minute or two. Suddenly, without a word, she darted out.

Thirty seconds later Mrs. Brady was elated to find two crumpled one-dollar bills lying in her saucer. Her joy, however, died a premature death. For she made an almost simultaneous second discovery. A saddening one. Above all, a puzzling one.

"Now what for," marveled Mrs. Brady, "did she want to walk off with them *scissors*?"

This at twelve twenty-five.

At twelve-thirty a quartette of excited young things burst in, babbling madly. All of them had their evening wraps with them; all talked at once. One of them, a Dresden-china girl with a heart-shaped face, was the center of attraction.

Around her the rest fluttered like monstrous butterflies; to her they addressed their shrill exclamatory cries. "Babe," they called her.

Mrs. Brady heard snatches: "Not in this state unless…" "Well, you can in Maryland, Jimmy says." "Oh, there must be some place nearer than…" "Isn't this *marvelous*?" "When did it happen, Babe? When did you decide?"

"Just now," the girl with the heart-shaped face sang softly, "when we were dancing."

The babble resumed, "But listen, Babe, what'll your mother and father?…" "Oh, never mind, let's hurry." "Shall we be warm enough with just these thin wraps, do you think? Babe, will you be warm enough? Sure?"

Powder flew and little pocket combs marched through bright marcels. Flushed cheeks were painted pinker still.

"My pearls," said Babe, "are *old*. And my dress and my slippers are new. Now, let's see—what can I *borrow*?"

A lace handkerchief, a diamond bar pin, a pair of earrings were proffered. She chose the bar pin, and its owner unpinned it proudly, gladly.

"I've got blue garters!" exclaimed a shrill little girl in a silver dress.

"Give me one, then," directed Babe. "I'll trade with you… There! That fixes that."

More babbling, "Hurry! Hurry up!"… "Listen, are you *sure* we'll be warm enough? Because we can stop at my house, there's nobody home." "Give me that puff, Babe,

I'll powder your back.'" "And just to think a week ago you'd never even met each other!" "Oh, hurry *up*, let's get *started*!" "I'm ready." "So'm I." "Ready, Babe? You look adorable." "Come on, everybody."

They were gone again, and the dressing room seemed twice as still and vacant as before.

A minute of grace, during which Mrs. Brady wiped the spilled powder away with a damp gray rag. Then the door jumped open again. Two evening gowns appeared and made for the dressing table in a bee line. Slim tubular gowns they were, one silver, one palest yellow. Yellow hair went with the silver gown, brown hair with the yellow. The silver-gowned, yellow-haired girl wore orchids on her shoulder, three of them, and a flashing bracelet on each fragile wrist. The other girl looked less prosperous; still, you would rather have looked at her.

Both ignored Mrs. Brady's cosmetic display as utterly as they ignored Mrs. Brady, producing full field equipment of their own.

"Well," said the girl with orchids, rouging energetically, "how do you like him?"

"Oh-h—all right."

"Meaning, 'Not any,' hmm? I suspected as much!" The girl with orchids turned in her chair and scanned her companion's profile with disapproval. "See here, Marilee," she drawled, "are you going to be a damn fool *all* your life?"

"He's fat," said Marilee dreamily. "Fat, and—greasy, sort of. I mean, greasy in his mind. Don't you know what I mean?"

"I know *one* thing," declared the other. "I know Who He Is! And if I were you, that's all I'd need to know. *Under the circumstances.*"

The last three words, stressed meaningly, affected the girl called Marilee curiously. She grew grave. Her lips and lashes drooped. For some seconds she sat frowning a little, breaking a black-sheathed lipstick in two and fitting it together again.

"She's worse," she said finally, low.

"Worse?"

Marilee nodded.

"Well," said the girl with orchids, "there you are. It's the climate. She'll never be anything *but* worse, if she doesn't get away. Out West, or somewhere."

"I know," murmured Marilee.

The other girl opened a tin of eye shadow. "Of course," she said dryly, "suit yourself. She's not *my* sister."

Marilee said nothing. Quiet she sat, breaking the lipstick, mending it, breaking it.

"Oh, well," she breathed finally, wearily, and straightened up. She propped her elbows on the plate-glass dressing-table top and leaned toward the mirror, and with the lipstick she began to make her coral-pink mouth very red and gay and reckless and alluring.

*

Nightly at one o'clock Vane and Moreno dance for the Club Français. They dance a tango, they dance a waltz; then, by way of encore, they do a Black Bottom, and a trick of their own called the Wheel. They dance for twenty, thirty minutes. And while they dance you do not leave your table—for this is what you came to see. Vane and Moreno. The new New York thrill. The sole justification for the five-dollar couvert extorted by Billy Costello.

From one until half-past, then, was Mrs. Brady's recess. She had been looking forward to it all the evening long. When it began—when the opening chords of the tango music sounded stirringly from the room outside—Mrs. Brady brightened. With a right good will she sped the parting guests.

Alone, she unlocked her cupboard and took out her magazine—the magazine she had bought three hours before. Heaving a great breath of relief and satisfaction, she plumped herself on the couch and fingered the pages. Immediately she was absorbed, her eyes drinking up printed lines, her lips moving soundlessly.

The magazine was Mrs. Brady's favorite. Its stories were true stories, taken from life (so the editor said); and to Mrs. Brady they were live, vivid threads in the dull, drab pattern of her night.

THE CHICAGO KID:
A STORY OF CABARET LIFE

Gertrude Schalk

National News, March 24th 1932

T HE DRESSING ROOM was in an uproar. Mazie vainly trying to make herself heard, finally waved the telegram over her head and shouted:

"Willya shut up for one minute!"

Gradually the voices softened while six wide-eyed girls gathered around.

"Honest, Mazie, did the High-Flyer really marry that foreign millionaire?" The girl from Chicago begged for an answer. "I saw it in the papers, but you can't believe…"

"If you'll wait a minute while I read her telegram…" Mazie said witheringly. Flora shut up, her lovely brown skin tinted with pink from the excitement. "Bobbie says, 'Sorry I couldn't give notice, but Juan is so impatient. Married this morning. Love, Bobbie.' Then," Mazie grinned faintly, "she added a P.S. 'Who said I wouldn't touch the sky!'"

There was an undercurrent of excitement all through the Yellow Parrot that evening. Even the patrons were thrilled with the romance of the little chorus girl who had nabbed the hitherto girl-shy millionaire. Every time the girls came out there was an extra round of applause.

Jinks, the manager, was part angry, part pleased. Angry because Bobbie had left an empty space in the chorus. Pleased, because it had given extra publicity to the Yellow Parrot to have her elope with Juan.

And the girls… of course they were filled with envy. Not badly but just enough to make them wistful. Only Flora, the kid from Chicago, took it hard.

"Hot Damn!" she swore softly to herself once while she was repairing her make-up between numbers. "I'm better looking than Bobbie. I can dance better. I got more personality. Why couldn't I have married that guy?"

It began to gall her horribly. Why hadn't she seen him first? Believe it or not, if she had seen him first, he'd never have even sneered at the High-Flyer! Why her figure could beat that bean's stringiness any day of the week!

It did something to her native cautiousness, this coup of Bobbie's. So that later in the evening when a loud party of down-towners spilled into the night club and began getting wise with the girls, Flora dimpled demurely and smiled back. They spelled money to her knowing eyes. That older man with the gray eyes and iron-gray hair… well, you just know he owned a couple of banks and a flock of apartment houses.

It was Jinks, unknowingly, who put the final dot to the decision that had been forming slowly behind Flora's curly head. He came into the dressing room between numbers and gave a "pep" talk.

"Listen, girls," he rubbed his hands together (denoting good business) and beamed. "There's our first real big money party out there now! What I mean BIG money! John Martin who owns half the land in New York state and a couple other states besides… anyway, he's out there with a party. And I want you kids to do your stuff!"

Flora narrowed her eyes thoughtfully and grinned. Here was her chance made to order. Other chorus girls landed rich white men, why shouldn't she? Why, look at the girls who drove their own Packards and who had three or four coats! They didn't get them off no measly fifty per week. Huh!

Flora was easily the best looker in the chorus. But this evening she was twice as hot looking. Her eyes sparkled overtime; her lips were too luscious and red; her bare shoulders gleamed softly brown under the changing lights. And behind all that lay a great purpose.

John Martin wasn't as drunk as the rest of his party, but he was gay enough to try and flirt with Flora. In fact whether he knew it or not, it was Flora who paved the way for the little byplay that came about at the end of a certain number.

To all appearances it was just an accident, but Flora knew that by giving an extra wide turn at the end, she could make herself half slide into John Martin's lap! She did, and of course, he held her tight for one little moment.

Just long enough for her to melt softly into his lap in a sort of velvety bundle that sent tiny prickles of feeling darting thru his body…

Then she was gone, her lovely legs twinkling across the floor, her arms outstretched, an audacious twinkle in her dark eyes.

Back in the dressing room Flora nodded to her reflection in the mirror. "That ought to bring him, baby!" she told herself softly.

The next time she danced out into the spotlight, a demure, holier-than-thou expression in her wide eyes, Flora didn't even glance John Martin's way. Not even when he pursed his lips and made a soft hissing sound. She merely danced past, eyes straight ahead and let him whistle.

But once back in the dressing room, Flora scuttled to where she could peep unseen into the club proper. John Martin was looking around arrogantly, his eyes seeking…

Jinks came over bowing profoundly. Martin beckoned him closer, whispered in the manager's ear.

Flora shivered with excitement. If Jinks headed for the dressing room, she'd know for sure that she had attracted John "Million-bucks" Martin!

And while she jiggled there nervously, Flora saw Jinks straighten up, grin knowingly and then wheel to march straight toward her!

None of the girls knew just why Flora flew to her chair and proceeded to be very busy making up when Jinks walked in. But they did know something was up when he bent over Flora's chair and did a powerful lot of whispering in her ear.

"He wants to meet you, kid," Jinks told her.

"Nothing doing," Flora pretended indifference.

"Ah, say... give him a play for the night anyway. He means money!"

"Sorry," Flora patted a bit more powder on her nose. "I didn't know we were supposed to be nice to the customers..."

"Hell, yes! What you think..." Jinks was mad now, growing red in queer patches around his neck. "You treat him nice, get me? I mean while you're working. Outside, 'taint none of my business, see?"

Flora nodded shortly. Inwardly she was gloating. Just what she wanted. Jinks's approval. With a casual air she sauntered out into the club, ignoring the curiosity glowing in Mazie's eyes.

This was one doll that Mazie wasn't going to have any hand in her business!

John Martin was very polite when Jinks introduced them. He complimented her on her dancing and then, on the verge of leaving, he shook hands and in shaking... left a card lying in Flora's palm.

Later, in the semi-privacy of the dressing room, she read the two lines of writing.

"I'll be expecting you for dinner tomorrow at seven."

And below, his address on Park Avenue!

Flora was thrilled, triumphant. Who said she wouldn't get herself a millionaire! She mightn't get a wedding ring with him—but who wanted one of them halters in these days and times! People got tired of seeing the same folks around day after day, year after bunk anyway. But money… having that was all to the good! And she was on her way.

The next morning Flora woke early. She just couldn't sleep for thinking about John Martin and the dinner date. He must like her a lot to ask her to dinner in his own apartment! Park Avenue… cripes!

She fussed and she fumed getting ready. She changed from the black satin dress to the dark blue crepe and then back again, until finally when the clock pointed to six o'clock, Flora dabbed once more at her face with the powder puff and dashed madly down the street.

She got into a taxi and then seeing the time, realized that she'd probably be too early for her appointment—and got out at the next corner. Ran over to Lenox and caught the "L." That would give her plenty of time to walk down Park Avenue…

It was just ten minutes past seven when Flora strolled nonchalantly into John Martin's dimly lighted, gorgeous penthouse.

"My dear!" Martin himself came eagerly forward to greet her, his finely kept hand held out to grip hers. "I'm so glad you could come."

"Thank you for having me," Flora smiled sweetly, let her lids droop, and then lifted them with bewildering swiftness. "But isn't it just grand... just lovely here!"

John Martin's hands quivered with some inner emotion, removing her coat, lifting it from her smooth, bare brown arms. Just two thin black satin straps in an expanse of velvety skin...

Flora pretended not to notice his nervousness, of the way his eyes kept wandering from her face...

After all it wasn't so different from half a hundred other little dinners Flora had enjoyed in her brief life. Only the men in those cases had been just ordinary boys who worked around Chicago.

John Martin for all his money was an ordinary man as far as Flora could see. He laughed at the same jokes, pulled the same dumb line, even tried to hold hands under the table and play footy-footy!

Brothers under the skin, Flora thought humorously, remembering a yellow boy who had done the same thing not many moons ago. What was color, money, position when a girl is involved!

After dinner—Flora knew it was coming then—the proposition. No doubting it after getting a good look at Martin's twitching lips. He was off the deep end already. And of course she knew what she was going to say and do. Drive a bargain, her brain told her shrewdly. Don't trust to chance or promise. Get something definite and hang on to it!

Martin drew her down on one of those modernistic, backless divans so deep and soft, Flora grew breathless from sinking down, down into it. And then suddenly he had her in his arms and his damp, loose lips were slipping over her face, her neck... his hand was sliding the little strap down over the golden brown shoulder...

Flora endured it, holding her breath, closing her eyes. A bit worse than she expected, but then... you can't have everything. You can't expect a perfect lover and a millionaire daddy to be rolled up in the same package.

"You beautiful little thing..." he was whispering huskily. He pressed closer, his hands almost burning her with their heat. His hands... hard not to shudder when they passed so intimately over her scantily clad body. But remember the millions...

And then when it seemed most anything might happen... when a scream was just bitten behind her tongue... Flora heard another woman's voice, thick with anger, shouting loudly!

John Martin started, sat up and then tried clumsily to jump to his feet. Difficult to do when the divan was so low and so downy. After two ludicrous efforts he made it and turned to face the door.

"You thought I wouldn't know, you two-timer!" The woman who had been standing in the door advanced into the room. Flora, sitting up now, recognized her as one of the party of the night before. A tall blonde, rather hard faced, but pretty. "Listen," she went on harshly, "you old coot, who do you think you are double-crossing anyway? Not little Peggy!"

John Martin stammered, hemmed and hawed, tried to look dignified, failing each time. Flora, for the moment unnoticed, edged over until she could drop lightly over the edge of the divan onto the floor. For she had seen what she had seen! Nothing less than an automatic in the determined hand of Peggy!

"Now, Peggy my dear," Martin was saying, "There must be some mistake. I wouldn't double-cross you…"

"Not much!" Peggy retorted. "Every time you think my back's turned, you dig up another dame. And now you've gone shady on me. Got to have you a tanned mama—oh yeah?"

And then she whirled, faced Flora. "Hey you, come here and step on it!" She sneered then. "Lemme look at you."

And that's where she made her mistake!

Until then Flora had been scared. But when blond Peggy had said those few words…

Flora got up, sauntered over, her hands on her hips. No one to tell Peggy that when the kid from Chicago put her hands on her hips it was time to be pulling out. Anyway, Flora was half a head shorter than Peggy and Peggy had a gun.

"Listen, Harlem." Peggy seemed to be enjoying it now. "This bozo happens to be my meal ticket and rent money.

So lay off, get it? Not that there's much chance of him picking you…"

"Just a minute—" Flora took another step forward. "Before I flatten that skinny nose of yours, who do you think you're talking to?"

Flora's voice as silky as a baby's, but behind it… boy!

Peggy brought her hand up, holding the gun tight. "Getting tight on me, baby?" she hissed, narrowing her eyes.

"Oh yeah!" Flora's hand flashed out. There was a scream, a scuffling of two sets of silk encased limbs… a scrambling of hands and arms combined with John Martin's gasping:

"Girls… please, girls… stop… don't… you mustn't!"

Ten minutes later Flora shrugged into her coat, dabbed a bit of powder on her nose and kicked one of Peggy's shoes sky high. Behind the divan the blond beauty shivered and cried, the while trying to hold together the pieces of what had once been an exceedingly pretty… and expensive… gown.

"And let this be a lesson to you," Flora remarked calmly as she walked out. And there beside the elevator stood John Martin, admiration glowing in his eyes.

With a hasty look over his shoulder at the door of his house, he took Flora's reluctant hand, pressed something in the palm.

"Baby, it was worth lots more, but that's all I have with me now!" he whispered. "I've been wanting to do that for months!"

He tiptoed back into the penthouse, closed the door, leaving Flora staring wide eyed at a fat wad of bills that lay in her hand.

It wasn't until she was in a taxi going back up town that Flora really came out of the daze that had come over her. With eager fingers she hid the roll of bills, her eyes glistening, thinking of all the pretty things she could buy now... No millionaire to buy them for her though. At least, not at present. Millionaires, it seemed, weren't to be had just for the taking, even when they were willing to be taken:

"Hasn't been such a bad night," Flora told herself, patting the lump that was a wad of greenbacks. "Pretty profitable to say the least. Only..." A tinge of regret showing for a moment in her eyes. "If I had known he was going to pay me for beating her up, instead of sending for the cops... I'd have socked her another couple on that skinny nose!"

NOT THE MARRYING KIND

Dawn Powell

Snappy Stories, March 1927

A ILEEN HAD ON a black chiffon frock that reached exactly to her knees. Every time she Charlestoned by with Dan Tracy, the chaperons, with one accord, lowered their eyes.

"The jeweled garters showing is bad enough," gasped the oldest chaperon, "but, my dear, those ruffles! I saw them distinctly."

"She's not the sort of girl men marry," said the second oldest chaperon, waggling a palm leaf fan. "You mark my words, she'll be an old maid!"

With this satisfactory conclusion the four chaperons of the High Water Club adjourned for a little punch—properly stiffened with gin—and sixty couples disappeared from the veranda in sixty different directions.

Aileen Merrick, comfortably leaning on Dan Tracy's shoulder in the Italian garden, would have shocked the chaperons far more if they could have heard her.

"This is all very pretty, Dan," she observed, "but it doesn't mean a darn thing. Why don't you really fall in love with me? I'm awfully nice."

Dan casually kissed her left eye.

"Very likely I might have made a fool of myself over you, Aileen," he retorted amiably, "if you weren't so damned modern."

"You mean I don't look like first mortgages and linen showers and Ludwig Baumann's," Aileen thoughtfully helped him out. "I'm your party gal."

"Rhinestone heels and champagne and orchids," Dan waved a cigarette, "and how. Awful good company but not a good wife."

"If you're looking for the marrying kind," Aileen said demurely, "I'm surprised you haven't picked on Joan Marble."

"Thanks," Tracy languidly replied. "I may do it yet. Let me give you a light."

And two hours later Aileen, who had firmly decided to go home in Dan Tracy's new sedan, experienced a faint shock. She saw Dan leading Joan Marble, cloaked and smiling, out to the carriage entrance. Very jauntily Aileen walked over to the Delfords' car and announced that they were to have the pleasure of taking her home.

"My dear," gurgled Freda Delford, upon whose lap she was very uncomfortably ensconced, "do you know what

Tess told me as we were leaving? Dan Tracy and Joan went off together!"

"Shall it be a cut-glass punch bowl or sherbet glasses this time, darling?" chanted Jimmy Delford.

"Silly!" laughed Freda. "But you know it's true that when you see Joan with a man it means something. Might as well pick their wedding present right away."

Aileen forced a laugh. Her face looked a little pinched in the glare of the street lamps, but that may have been the cold night wind.

"You ran around a good deal with Dan this winter, didn't you, Aileen?" asked Jimmy. "Seems to me I used to be forever bumping into you two holding hands out in my car between dances."

"Very likely," admitted Aileen. "Dan's a swell hand-holder... Here we are at the old homestead, Jimmy, and if you knock that post over again the janitor will kill you."

She wriggled past Freda's very plump knees, jumped to the ground and caught her white Spanish shawl on the brakes. It ripped obligingly and Aileen muttered a very gentle "damn."

"That's all right, Aileen," Freda giggled. "You'll sell enough houses tomorrow to buy a new evening wrap. Night!"

"Don't forget to razz Dan about Joan if you see him," Jimmy called. "There's sure to be something serious on."

Aileen stumbled across the sidewalk, and up the front steps, the torn fringe trailing. The new maid let her in the front door, and looked at her in disapproval. Miss Merrick was certainly staggering, and moreover she was laughing to herself in the most grotesque fashion. The new maid concluded instantly that what the town people had told her was true—Miss Merrick drank… But it wasn't the drink from Jimmy's flask that made Aileen laugh. It had suddenly struck her as superbly amusing that she and Dan Tracy should play around all season without Glendale batting an eye; whereas he had only to take Joan Marble home once from a dance and the town was agog.

"Must be I'm an awfully harmless soul," Aileen thought ruefully. "Ugh! How ghastly!"

Taking Joan home that night was a purely accidental gesture for Dan. His rooms were not far from the Marble residence, and when he saw Joan slipping out of the dressing room all alone there was only one thing to be done. They didn't exchange a dozen words in the ride home, yet Dan found he had a date with Joan for the following Sunday, and an apparently permanent date for the Saturday afternoon concert series at Music Hall.

Dan really was puzzled as to how it had happened. Joan had certainly not been forward. He himself was such an informal soul—never called a girl up till the last minute, and usually he just dropped in. Yet here he was with a string of definite engagements with one girl.

"Still, I need to know a girl like Joan Marble," he finally reflected. "A real woman. Nothing flighty about Joan. Sweet, too. And old-fashioned. You don't have the feeling that tomorrow night she'll be kissing somebody else…"

Dan was close to thirty and had been perilously close to marrying Aileen. After all, he would soon be making enough for two, and an architect needn't worry about getting on… that is, if he was the only one in town, as Dan was in Glendale. And a man needed someone… a little house, say, on the Club Boulevard… a couple of collies, and, oh, I don't know, things of his own. Substantial, permanent things. The trouble was that women weren't the right sort anymore. Aileen was a good pal, but she was entirely self-sufficient. If he chanced to be in a sentimental mood—and Dan admitted having sentimental moods—it was just like Aileen to get hilariously lit, or to ask his advice about some problem in her exceedingly successful real-estate business.

Somehow you couldn't picture Aileen Merrick as the sweet, demure wife of a struggling young architect, acting as hostess to possible clients, helping him in the subtle fashion of old-fashioned wives to get ahead in his business. That was Joan Marble. Aileen, now… Dan's mouth twisted in a grin. It would be more like Aileen to reveal complete and utter boredom to his precious clients and then to relieve that boredom by getting potted.

That was Aileen. And Dan had just about decided it was time to stop idling with these modern young women, time to take root, so to speak. He'd look around a while, first, of course, and when he'd made up his mind…

He sent Joan a dozen roses on Sunday. When he called he found Joan in soft blond lace thoughtfully arranging the flowers in a Chinese bowl. The wood fire was burning, as it did in the Marble living room almost every Sunday the year round, and it spread an inviting glow over the tea wagon, set with tea things. Dan's grave face brightened at the picture. How much jollier than the chattering Sunday mob in Aileen's living room!

"It wasn't necessary to send the roses, Dan," Joan said in her soft voice, coming up to take his hand. "And wasn't it the least little bit extravagant for a young man who's just bought a rather expensive car?"

"Flowers are necessities for beautiful ladies," Dan protested, sinking into the grateful depths of the armchair. "I've given up candy as a tribute, now that all you girls are reducing. Anyway, those roses look slick the way you have them in that Chinese dingus."

Joan sat down at the tea wagon.

"I'd rather not have the candy" she smiled. "It always seems a pity to me that these tributes as you call them should be perishable. For my part I can't help thinking of the perfectly ravishing candlesticks that could be bought with that money, or the books, or—well, things that will last."

"I'll remember that, henceforth," Dan answered.

Joan Marble was a wholesome girl contrasted with the usual type of modern young woman, Dan thought, as she poured the tea. She made up only a little, and she had preserved her long fair hair through the whole bobbing epidemic. It coiled on her graceful white neck and made a gleaming mellow line about her smooth white face.

Dan wondered why he had never noticed Joan before. She had gone to boarding school and the university with Aileen's set, he knew, but she came only occasionally to their parties. She never drank nor smoked, and she seemed well liked in the town. He tried to remember what he had heard of her. She'd been engaged once or twice, but the affair had been broken off each time through no fault of Joan's. Joan had been bewildered and dazed after each fiasco. Aileen had said something about her once. Dan tried to remember… Oh, yes…

"There's something about Joan Marble. At the university, the rest of us girls used to wear a man's fraternity pin for a year and never think it was anything serious. But the minute you'd see Joan walking across the campus with a man, everybody would start sewing doilies for Joan's hope chest. Somehow she simply radiated marriage and dotted Swiss curtains and bungalow aprons and shopping for the nicest of fresh vegetables and no-babies-the-first-year-but-of-course-eventually—and that old substantial stuff… And even if it was a new man every year, you never thought of Joan as a flirt. You had only to look at that sweet, womanly face to know that it was really serious."

Dan wondered a little why Joan had never married. You never wondered that about Aileen. They were the same age, too, around twenty-two or -three. But Joan was so obviously the marrying kind. She lived at home with her father and an aunt, and did nothing beyond a little welfare stuff out in the mill section. She expected to marry, of course. Aileen and Freda used to joke about Joan's hope chest. At Christmas Joan always asked people not to give her perfumes and things like that, but spoons or linen or something for her hope chest… What had happened to the men she'd been engaged to, Dan wondered.

"Do you mind handing me that sewing bag?" Joan asked, pushing the wagon to one side and slipping into a low chair beside Dan. "I can work while you tell me all about yourself."

"No time to be wasted in merely listening," bantered Dan.

"Please don't think that," begged Joan. "I do want to hear, but I listen so much better when my hands are busy. This is my twelfth. Isn't that nice?"

"Twelfth what?" Dan asked blankly, and then saw that she meant her twelfth guest towel. He began to explain why he had happened to choose Glendale of all the little Westchester towns he might have picked. While he talked Joan sewed quietly. It was a very restful evening. Somehow Dan found he was expected every Sunday evening from now on for tea. Joan was awfully sweet. She seemed to absorb his words and muse vaguely over them as one, who, pathetically enough, has little to muse on beyond what thoughts are brought to her by her occasional men callers. When Dan had finished his last anecdote of the architectural business in Glendale, Joan looked up at him with a dreamy, far-away gaze.

"Hasn't it been a lovely evening?" she exclaimed. "Just look! I've finished my dozen. Tomorrow I can start on pillow slips."

Aileen told herself she didn't care. Fancy eating one's heart out for a man in this day and age! She'd just like to see the one who could put a crimp in her life!… Only it was sort of queer not seeing Dan Tracy around her apartment any more. Coming in from a gorgeous tiring day of selling lots—and she did sell 'em—in Beach Parkway, and finding old Dan making himself at home in her little place.

"Aileen," he would say, "you ought to be spanked for leaving this place the way you do! Here I get so chesty to Bodley—he ran down today—"

"Not Bodley?" Aileen's gray eyes widened in horror. "Don't tell me you brought him up?"

"I did," Dan declared virtuously. "You said you wanted to meet him—the famous Bodley—and I dragged him up here to meet the Fascinating Flapper Realtor of Westchester, and incidentally to have a nip from your cellarette."

"And the maid's gone," Aileen gurgled, dropping on the sofa. "And the bed wasn't made, and I'd left the glasses all over the way they were after the party! Oh, Dan! How killing! And he might even tell Aunt Bertha!"

At which Dan looked at her half-reproachfully and half-amused.

"I had to chase Bodley away… I wanted to clean up, but where do you keep your broom?"

"There isn't any," explained Aileen cheerfully. "I always forget to get one. I just sort of dust around. When I get a maid again, she'll have to bring her own broom. Don't look that way, Dan. I need a—a wife, I guess, to look after me. Or maybe I'd better have Aunt Bertha come out from town. How she'd love it!"

There never had been anyone like Dan Tracy, Aileen was sure. To begin with he was that dark, ugly, keen sort that women always found utterly irresistible. You felt the tremendous strength and paradoxical delicacy that was in him as soon as you looked into his dark eyes. A man who could make love as casually as any other young man in the Glendale younger set, but each time he lightly kissed her Aileen hungered to know what it would be like if he really loved one… Aileen didn't intend to let her merry life be messed up by taking men and love too seriously, but if there ever should be a man, there was a tiny, irrepressible wish that it might be Dan Tracy.

And now he was probably going to marry Joan Marble. And that was that! Aileen took care to smile brilliantly at the two every time she saw them together—and Glendale saw them frequently together that spring.

"Aileen, you know Dan better than anyone else," begged Freda Delford one afternoon—it was at Jen Terry's bridge—"will he really marry Joan?"

"Does anyone ever marry Joan?" Aileen countered, with faint malice. She was not playing, but stood leaning against the porch pillar, her late pallor accentuated by the bright dabs of tangerine rouge in the hollows of her cheeks. Her pleated geranium silk hung on her a little limply... the girls said she was working too hard, but wasn't it grand, though, to be so thin?

"That's true," said Freda thoughtfully. "We always say Joan is different—the marrying sort—but she never actually got to the altar, did she? Why, how many men did she get engaged to since freshman year at U? There was Arty Maxwell, first. We gave her the linen shower I remember. Only he didn't come back to college the next year—"

"And Don Reed, and Mark Blaine, and Fred Wright," contributed Marjorie Delford, Jimmy's young sister.

"Joan was always constant," Aileen commented. "It was only her fiancé who varied."

"I don't think Joan ever looked up from her embroidery long enough to know who the man was, anyway," Marjorie burst out. "He was simply Husband to Joan. I don't think she gave a whoop who he was or what. Just Mate—that was all."

"She's that kind that envelop men in marriage without ever doing a darn thing," Freda reflected.

"Mark Blaine stuck nearly a year," Aileen said, staring absently across the lawn. She knew that presently Dan would drive past on his way home from his Saturday trip to New York. "They say he really loved Joan, only he got the idea she was merely in love with the matrimonial system and not with Mark Blaine at all. He ran off to South America, don't you remember? Joan couldn't understand it at all. But in a month or two she was working monograms on the sheets for her hope chest just because Shorty Briggs had asked her to go to the movies."

"Sh—sh—there goes Dan's car!" hissed Freda.

Aileen strained her eyes. Dan waved to the group on the porch and Aileen waved languidly back. Nothing in her young life if a man wanted to be the dummy in some eager bride's hope chest. She could have a good time without Dan.

Old Mrs. Terry waddled out on the porch. She, too, wanted to talk about dear Mr. Tracy and sweet little Joan.

"A splendid wife for Dan Tracy," she exclaimed.

"Dan's too poor to marry," Aileen said abruptly. "At least for a while."

"Never mind," breathed Mrs. Terry amiably. "Joan is a fine little manager. She's just the kind to manage well.

There's no nonsense to Joan… not like the rest of you girls, let me tell you!"

"Now, grandma!" protested Jen, but the old lady paid no heed.

"You don't see Joan going to offices and running around in these knickers and trying to act like a man," Mrs. Terry's head wagged significantly toward Aileen. "Dresses up to her knees and no petticoats—no indeed, not Joan. Joan's the kind of girl I used to be when I was young—and your grandma, Freda, was just the same. Girls had no thought then but to make some man a good wife."

"Some man—you mean any man," impudently retorted her granddaughter.

"Joan's all right," Freda soothed the old lady. "It isn't her fault if she missed her entrance by about eighty years."

"A dear sweet girl." muttered Mrs. Terry, and sank into a wicker chair with a sigh. "And just the wife for that nice young man."

Aileen snatched her hat and walked down to her waiting roadster. She couldn't stand the talk any longer. Why in the name of mercy couldn't she get Dan Tracy out of her head? If she had to be worrying about something, she ought to worry about how to sell the old Riggs estate, instead of some other girl's man… A few kisses after a dance—leaning against his shoulder one night faint with the pain of a twisted ankle—the memories of his dark, brooding eyes… Aileen yanked the door of the car shut.

"What the hot place!" she said defiantly, and stepped on the gas.

Dan was slightly dazed on finding himself just five weeks from his wedding day. He didn't remember how the thing had happened. He knew it was a frightfully good thing—oh, an excellent thing for a young architect to be married—and he knew that Joan Marble would make any man a splendid wife. But the exact connection between these two facts somehow escaped his memory. He only knew now that he and Joan spent their evenings going over house plans and making budgets and things.

After the first shock had worn off Dan began to feel rather pleased with this painless settling of his future. It seemed such a wise and sensible thing to do. Exactly what he had thought of only last year as the ideal step for a man just thirty.

"I don't think we ought to wait till fall, dear," Joan said one evening, as she bent over the intricate embroidery pattern of a table cloth. "I thought the tenth of July."

Dan brought himself up with a start. The tenth of July? Somehow July seemed perilously near. He hadn't thought of the affair as quite so imminent. It was only a month off. Good Heavens!

"But, Joan!" he exclaimed in a panic. "I don't think you understand. I'm really frightfully poor. I only made three thousand last year, and while I have the church contract, I won't get the money till next January. Honestly, Joan—"

"I can manage," Joan said tranquilly, snipping a thread with her teeth. Dan experienced a sudden annoyance with her eternal embroidering and snipping. You talked to Joan's hair all the time.

What had started their engagement in the first place? There had been no actual proposal. They had drifted into talking about marriage in the abstract—there seemed nothing else to talk about to Joan—and quite suddenly it began to be *their* marriage and not the institution. The naturalness of it bothered Dan a little. He felt rather cheated—slipping into matrimony almost without any choice on his part. He gazed soberly down at Joan's smooth fair hair.

"But, Joan, you don't understand," he repeated patiently. "I'm sure you could manage on a small income. But you see I won't have a cent till November. I'd have to borrow to furnish our apartment"

"I know, dear," said Joan, and this time she looked up into his eyes. "But I have my hope chest."

"Hope chest?" repeated Dan stupidly.

Joan's eyes began to shine. A smile played about her lips.

"Do you know, Danny," she said in a soft elation, "I have eight dozen tablecloths, twelve dozen napkins, eleven pairs of blankets, nine dozen pillow slips, five dozen sherbet glasses, six mayonnaise bowls, four dozen dessert spoons, twenty-three dresser scarfs—"

"But, good Lord, Joan," Dan cried, his jaw dropping, "we've only been engaged since May!"

"I know, dear," Joan said triumphantly. "But you see I started this chest when I was ten, thirteen years ago, so that I would always be ready for my wedding."

She stood there glowing at him, but Dan's face was heavy. He felt hopeless. He was a mere atom in a vast system. He had been fated to inherit that hope chest all of his life. When he had been a blithe child, innocently unsuspecting, strands of blue silk were being woven into dresser scarves against his coming. When he had started gaily off to college, wondering what the years would hold for him, Joan was sitting at home, her head bent, patiently weaving—weaving his future into her embroidery pattern. While he was idly speculating as to whether or not he should marry someone, Joan was waiting with tranquil, certain eyes.

"I was caught before I had even begun to run," Dan groaned inwardly. "Good Heavens, I can't marry someone just because she's got her hope chest full. Hang it all, I want the woman to be in love with me. I'm damned if I'll be the abstract man for which her hope chest stands. I can't. I won't."

The thing obsessed him so, that he got up and reached for his hat. It enraged him to see Joan sitting there, her head bent over the latest item for the chest.

"I'm going, Joan," he said slowly. "I…"

Joan looked up at him, puzzled by the significance of his tone.

"Oh, dear," she breathed, her blue eyes moistening, "what have I done now? What *have* I done?"

She looked with grieved surprise as he went out.

"What have I done?" she repeated worriedly. "I wonder—"

She retrieved her embroidery silk from the floor.

"I wonder—one, two, three—I wonder—one, two, three—"

The luncheon set was almost finished.

Jimmy Delford was driving past as Dan emerged from the Marble home. His car slid to the curb.

"Out my way?" he invited.

Tracy stepped into the car. Jimmy shot a sidelong glance at his haggard face.

"Jimmy," Dan said in a tense, choked voice, "help me, for heaven's sake. I tell you I'm scared."

"You need air, old man," Jimmy recommended. "You look all ashy. I'll spin you around a little bit."

"Jimmy, you're married—" Dan leaned toward him earnestly—"do all women have these hope chest things?"

Jimmy laughed shortly.

"Not a chance, old fellow, not a chance. Girls nowadays have too many other things to think about. Hope chests and marriage are about as important to them as a dinner date."

"Marriage isn't the goal of their lives, then?"

"From hearing Freda's crowd talk I should say not," laughed Jimmy. "I gather they want all out of life they can get, and from the way they pity 'poor Freda' I judge marriage doesn't fill the bill. Why, I had to argue Freda out of a grand interior decorating business in New York before she could see marriage."

"And when she finally took you instead of the job, I suppose you felt pretty set up," Dan continued thoughtfully.

"I'll say so," Jimmy nodded. "I knew it was me she really wanted, then, you see, not marriage or just a man—but me! I had a time selling her the idea, too. A man's job."

Dan's head began to feel clearer. That weight—that ghastly hope chest off his heart! Joan would have to understand it couldn't go on. She could find someone else who answered her purpose. For himself it was marvelous to feel free again, to feel himself once more the man who chose his destiny rather than one who was caught in it.

"Come up to the house," urged Jimmy, slowing up in front of the Delford bungalow.

Dan followed him up the graveled path and into the house, eager to reestablish his old bachelor footing. Jimmy ran upstairs in search of Freda and the key to the cellar. Dan stood for a thoughtful moment in the doorway of the living room…

Aileen Merrick, in tweed knickers, her dark bobbed hair curled about her face, was curled up in a chair busy with a fountain pen and a black notebook. There was a smudge on her nose, and a faint frown on her forehead as she figured intently. Presently she looked up. Her faintly shadowed eyes widened a little.

"Hello," she said, with an effort at casualness. "Come on in… By the way, I sold the Riggs' place today, Dan."

"Good!" He sat down in the chair opposite. She went on with her figures, and in the relief of her cool, casual silence, Dan breathed a great sigh of freedom.

"Gee, Aileen, I'm glad to see you!" he said. "When you finish let's drive over to the Club. Got any cigarettes?"

Aileen tossed him a pack without looking up.

She was afraid that if she did, he would see the preposterous tears in her eyes.

THOU SHALT NOT KILLJOY

Viña Delmar

Snappy Stories, December 20th 1923

Hallington C. Bond at the age of twelve had disapproved of ice cream, moving pictures and lemon meringue pie. He had never touched dice, took on a sickly pallor at the sight of cigarettes and simply loved every minute that he spent in the schoolroom.

At eighteen he founded the Anti-Vice League of North Angle, and at twenty-four he was the grimmest, busiest reforming killjoy of the town. He disapproved of everything that gave anyone pleasure—especially blondes. He believed that it was his special mission in life to purify the world and he began with poor little North Angle. He closed the one motion picture house, he stopped Sunday Victrola playing throughout the town, and he gave Lady Nicotine a terrible battle. Hallington C. Bond and his crew of undertakers put the lid on everything—on everything, that is except Teddy Tremont. And Hallington disapproved greatly of

Teddy! Teddy had red hair, and you can imagine what a demoralizing influence red hair would be in a town like North Angle. Too, she had greenish gray eyes that sparkled every day—including the Sabbath and holy days—and a trim little figure that even the perfect Hallington C. Bond didn't quite loathe.

But the worst of it all was that Teddy Tremont did not stand in awe of Mr. Bond, first, because she had known him back in the day when he had objected to nothing— meaning before he could talk. Second, because one night when the moon hung low over North Angle and the little coo-coo birds had called plainly to each other, Hallington C. Bond had held Teddy in his arms and begged her to be his. Translated, this means that the flaming-haired beauty wore a perfectly proper engagement ring in the generally accepted location and walked to church with Hallington C. Bond.

But the date of the wedding was set somewhere in the millennium, for Hallington, the dear thing, had an income of only twenty-two dollars a week from his father's estate and he could not spare the time from his reforming to go to work. But he assured Teddy daily that something cheerful was bound to happen; the oil well he had invested in was going to spout Omega or Aunt Katherine was going to die young. So Teddy waited.

Hallington Bond was really not bad to look at. He was tall and rather thin, of course, that half-fed look is part of every reformer's equipment. But he had nice dark eyes and hair that would curl though he kept it half drowned to discourage it. Once by mistake Hallington smiled and Teddy discovered that he had a gorgeous set of white and shining teeth. Just between you and me and the cover design, Teddy cared a lot for Hallington, but she would have cared heaps more if he hadn't served his kisses with a neat garniture of cracked ice.

What Hallington saw in Teddy to love would be obvious to no one but a psychoanalyst. Apparently, he was not in love with what she termed her "wise cracks" nor could it have been her gay spirits, for Hallington was at war with gay spirits. Perhaps at the age of six when he had triumphantly carried the news that Teddy was playing truant from Sunday school, it had seeped into his tiny consciousness that Teddy needed a firm and righteous protector; and that now this beauteous thought was blossoming. Or it may have been that Hallington Bond somewhere in the ice house that he called his brain, cherished a weakness for "wise cracks" and red hair—you never can tell about those things.

One lovely morning Hallington's phone rang. It did that often so don't become alarmed. But this morning it was a trifle early. Hallington hustled from his bed and crossed the hall to the instrument. He might have had his phone installed at the side of his bed but to be comfortable is to be sinful.

"Hello," he snapped.

"Good morning, Hal, don't bark at me." It was, of course, the future Mrs. Bond.

"I didn't mean to, dear, I assure you," Hallington hastily apologized, "but I have just arisen."

"Are you in your pajamas?" Teddy wanted to know.

"Teddy, a thousand times I have requested you to choose your words—"

"No lecture now, Kid. I just asked you a simple question. Are you in your pajamas?"

"Teddy, I—"

"Are you?"

"Heavens. Yes!"

"Well, don't get peevish. I just thought that if you were I'd tell you to pull down your shade."

And then she clicked off. Such a fiancée for the man who was going to make America purer than Ivory Soap!

"Was that Theodora?" called Hallington's aunt.

"Yes."

"What did she want so early?"

"Eh-eh," Hallington hesitated a second and then replied, "She wanted to tell me how to keep my worst self hidden from my neighbors." Which really wasn't so bad coming from Hallington C. Bond.

Then the busy day began. There was the hotel register to be examined, illicit liquor to be hunted for, two newcomers in the town to be observed and Mrs. Sennet's daughter to be lectured for wearing a short skirt. Hallington C. Bond climbed wearily into his clothes. The life of a reformer is not all gin sampling—but most of it is.

Something accomplished, something done, at evening North Angle's energetic reformer turned his steps toward the Tremont house and Teddy.

As he entered she rose quickly and came toward him. In the brief instant that he permitted himself to regard Teddy's charms, he noticed that her Grade A ankles were encased in dangerously sheer hose and that her arms were undoubtedly bare.

"Oh, Hal, dear, I'm so excited," she bubbled, "Jimmy Greer—that boy I met in Boston last winter—is over at West Traymore and he's calling here tonight."

Hallington C. Bond raised his eyebrows, covered a well-shaped yawn and said, "Don't enthuse so, Teddy. It's mildly vulgar. Did you say this Greer person was coming here?"

"Yes, and you needn't pretend that you don't mind. I can see Old Lady Jealousy biting holes in you."

"I, jealous? My dear Teddy, jealousy is the tomb of affection, the grave of trust, the morgue of sincere love."

"Yes, and the natural emotion of a real man. Now, be jealous of Jimmy Greer or I'll never speak to you again."

"The penalty is tremendously extreme, dear girl, but the request is intensely repellent to my finer sensibilities."

And then Jimmy Greer arrived. You've seen him, everybody has. Well-tailored, straw-hatted—bubbling over with current slang and hand-picked, seedless compliments. He knew all the vaudeville headliners, hinted at "dirt he could dish" if so-and-so wasn't his dearest pal and spoke of Nazimova as a "good kid who knew how to sell her stuff."

Hallington took an early departure, knowing full well that he could trust Teddy with vaudeville's kid brother. He could, that much I will say for Teddy.

For two weeks, Jimmy Greer hung around West Traymore and made frequent trips into North Angle to see Miss Tremont. It might have annoyed Hallington greatly but just around that time Hallington C. Bond was bursting into the limelight with his latest reform movement, namely, the Prohibition of Seductive Perfume Aromas. Every newspaper in the country was printing news of Hallington Bond's perfume campaign and he and his little band of hearse drivers were busier than one-arm paper hangers suppressing sinful, sensuous perfumes.

"That's a great idea," Teddy Tremont complained, "Am I supposed to sprinkle camphor over my clothes or anoint myself with the juice of the royal onion?"

"Neither, my dear. All I ask is that you do not use this vile, hell-inspired liquid that fires the senses and creates havoc where peace and tranquillity belong."

Teddy sighed. "Oh, Hallington, my dear pleasure assassin, don't tell me that anything ever fired your senses. If so, what?"

Hallington registered dismay. "You are speaking in a manner most unbecoming to a young lady," he said, "and I trust you will rid yourself of that devil-made stuff called 'Lillith's Kiss.'"

"Devil-made? Does he get twelve dollars a bottle for all his stuff?"

That was only one distressing interview with Teddy, others followed. For Teddy developed an inexplicable passion for the *Hot Tamale*. Now, the *Hot Tamale* was a magazine of dubious character filled from cover to cover with ladies who forever fought losing battles for their honor. It was one of those books that describe in detail what a nice girl wouldn't even imagine, and this was the thing that Teddy Tremont actually liked.

"I would be reconciled, dear girl, if the stories were skillfully constructed," Hallington told her sorrowfully, "But from what I have heard they have no redeeming trait."

"They are very clever," Teddy insisted. "Take this for instance." Teddy opened the *Hot Tamale* and began reading aloud, "'His arms went tight about her and Gladys fought her passion with a fierceness that startled them both. She felt his warm breath on her cheek and a mad, soul-stirring desire swept over her to surrender to this primitive joy that had burst the dam of convention at last. His fingers twined about hers and she knew that he read surrender in her trembling, white hand. He led her toward his cabin and—'"

"Stop!" shrieked Hallington C. Bond.

"Why, you evil-minded thing," said Teddy, "They were husband and wife all the time."

"It makes no difference," Hallington blustered. "Those stories are rot. There is nothing to them, I could write one only half trying."

"You could?"

"Certainly."

"I don't believe it. Besides one is nothing. Perhaps by a superhuman effort you could imagine one tricky situation, but these authors are always thinking up new, thrilling things—and that takes brains."

"Look here, Teddy, I don't make wagers—it isn't gentle-manly—but I promise you that I can write three stories with novel ideas that would reduce these mad ravings to nothing."

"You can?"

"Yes, and with no effort," Hallington bragged.

"Hm, I'd like to see those stories."

"You will," Hallington promised.

Then the clock struck nine-thirty and Hallington kissed Teddy on the forehead and started for home. The next days were busy ones for Hallington. Two girls in North Angle dyed their hair, one smoked a cigarette and a Mr. and Mrs. John Smith registered at the hotel. Besides all this hubbub the Perfume Bill was up in Washington and Hallington was a popular guy. Added to this Teddy went to New York. Hallington objected that New York was no place for a young and attractive girl.

"Oh, yes, it is, dear. You'd be surprised," cooed Teddy—and went.

They wrote to each other every day and it certainly seemed that Teddy was having a grand time in the big city. Jimmy Greer called on her frequently and he took her to the Statue of Liberty, the Palais Royale and the Aquarium. Hallington was broadminded, he didn't object—much.

It is surprising that he had any time to object, for after his day's work was done there was a certain mysterious business with a dictionary and a thesaurus that held his attention far into the wee, small hours. If anyone had gazed over the shoulder of North Angle's famous reformer, strange words would have met the curious one's eyes. For Hallington C. Bond was specializing in "passionate kisses" and "bosoms that rose and fell" to say nothing of the "crimson marvel that was Ardrita Sinclair's mouth."

Often as he strung adjectives together a frown would ruffle the smoothness of his brow, and it didn't look as though Hallington was doing it with "no effort."

But one night, with a sigh of satisfaction, he regarded three neat little mountains of typewriting. Great Caesar's ghost! if anyone had ever seen the words at the top of these mountains. For one read, "When Satan Loved," the second simply murmured, "I'm Glad To See You're Back," but the third threw discretion to the winds and proclaimed itself "A Woman of Thirteen Loves."

Hallington patted them tenderly and helped them into a capacious envelope. There is nothing odd in the fact that Teddy Tremont removed them from this very same envelope the next day and smothered a desire to scream with laughter.

She read the first and a thoughtful expression crept into her eyes.

"'When Satan Loved,'" she murmured. "That's a darn tricky title."

She gathered the manuscripts together and flew with them to her room. She read each one over twice and her thoughtful expression grew several shades more thoughtful. If her dear betrothed could have seen her at the moment he perhaps would have been mildly concerned; but a glimpse of her an hour later would have turned the blood in his virtuous veins to iced Lipton's. For Teddy Tremont with a funny little smile on the "crimson marvel that was her mouth" entered the offices of the *Hot Tamale* magazine and submitted three stories. Each bore the legend "by H. Bond" but Teddy left her own address.

She was terribly excited after doing this and in no humor to receive a proposal; but no one had informed Jimmy Greer of her feelings so he chose that evening to tell her the joke about orange blossoms and parlor furniture. She listened as any lady would do under the circumstances but she gave him an emphatic no in answer.

"You'll be sorry," Jimmy modestly warned her. "I'm a good fellow, Ted, I'd be a better husband than old Bad News up in North Angle."

Which reminded Teddy of something. "Jimmy, do you know any newspaper people?" she asked.

"Yes, but hell! they don't make good wives."

"Forget Lohengrin for a few minutes and listen. I'm not going to marry you, and I'm not going to be a sister to you, but I may want to meet a newspaper fellow in a week or two."

"Where's the connection?"

"There isn't any, but stick around. You'll probably come in handy."

So Jimmy stuck around while Hallington Bond reformed North Angle, while Teddy Tremont enjoyed New York, and while Editor Roberts of the *Hot Tamale* read and actually liked H. Bond's trio of naughty tales.

And so it happened that one day Teddy received a letter from the esteemed Mr. Roberts. All three stories had been purchased, and a fascinating, pale green slip of paper fluttered into Teddy's lap. Mr. Roberts expressed a desire to meet the young author and his wording conveyed more than an idle curiosity. Teddy reached for the telephone and called Jimmy Greer.

"When can I meet that newspaper person?" she asked.

"What newspaper person?"

"I'm not particular but I have a good story for someone."

It has been my unhappy discovery that men don't always rush to fulfill a lady's slightest whim, and Teddy made the same discovery when she sent Jimmy Greer to dig her up a knight of the press.

But at last she sat face to face with Ernest King of a certain well-known paper and spilled him the news.

"Look here," she said, "there is a certain Hallington Bond who has received a lot of notice for his Anti-Perfume Campaign. In his part of the country he has shut up everything but the churches. He's against everything but funerals. He's so pure, he's disgusting. He never smiles, he thinks chewing gum is a dissipation and if you laugh, Hallington Bond will have you jailed. Now, get this, Mr. King, I have a check made out to him by the *Hot Tamale* magazine for material furnished them and I happen to know that it is mighty hot material."

A smile of joy spread over Ernest King's face. "Oh, boy! Can I see the check?"

The evidence was produced and King questioned Teddy some more.

He thanked her, returned to his office—and another career was wrecked.

By morning Hallington C. Bond was a joke.

"The Blue Law Reformer With a Side Line" shrieked the papers.

"Bond, Who Preaches Purity, Writes Salacious Literature for the *Hot Tamale*."

Teddy obligingly produced photographs, and a facsimile of the ruinous check informed everyone, including Hallington C. Bond, that he was a *Hot Tamale* author. The mention of Bond's Perfume Campaign became a signal for mirth, and vaudevillians pounced on it with their customary cruelty.

And while this went on Teddy Tremont sat in fear and trembling awaiting Bond's righteous wrath, but never a word came from her sinless sweetie. Now, like all women from Eve of Edenville on, she asked herself why she had done this dark and dastardly deed. She asked, but she knew the answer. It was simply that she was sick and tired of having a holier-than-thou man hanging around. She wanted him to come down from his sterilized perch. She wanted him to be relieved of that pious manner of his—but now he probably hated her, for Hallington stripped of purity was Samson with a French Clip.

And Teddy was awfully sorry, for after all, Hallington with a flask of reforms on his hip was better than no Hallington.

The original date set for the termination of her visit came and went and Teddy did not return. She couldn't stand seeing Hallington crushed and ashamed, the laughingstock of North Angle.

Then one day as she turned things over in her mind Hallington C. Bond came upon the scene.

"Hello," he said.

"Why—why, Hal, aren't you mad at me?"

"Where's Jimmy Greer?" he asked abruptly.

"I haven't seen him in days, honestly I haven't."

"I've been in New York a week," Hallington said, "but I hesitated to look you up. I thought perhaps Jimmy Greer was filling your horizon."

"Gosh, Hal, he couldn't even fill my pipe if I smoked one."

Hallington C. Bond smiled. "Do you mean it?" he asked. "I was terribly jealous of him."

Teddy gazed wonderingly at him.

"Teddy, will you marry me now—today?"

"Why, Hallington, don't you understand, I've killed your chances to reform the world. I made you a sap to your own gang."

"I don't care, Ted."

"Really?"

"Honestly."

He held one of her hands tightly in his and Teddy felt very cozy and glad.

"But, Hal, conditions are the same. The well didn't shoot oil, did it?"

Hallington turned away and smiled a slow, shamefaced smile. "No, it didn't dear, but I've—I've contracted with the *Hot Tamale* to write twenty stories and it's pretty good money. Will you, dear?"

Hallington put his arms about her and held her close, and Teddy laughed a happy, little snicker into his shoulder.

"Hal, dear, I like you to kiss me but the man in that window over there is watching us."

"To hell with him," said Hallington C. Bond.

THE BRIDE OF BALLYHOO

Guy Gilpatric

College Humor, January 1929

W HEN THE ENGINE QUIT AND my left wing hit that Ferris wheel, I said to myself, "Well, here we go now!" Next thing I smelt a hospital, and I opened my eyes and sure enough it was.

I was still groggy and I hurt all over. There were a lot of hospital people standing around, and the head doctor told me I had crashed my plane. I said yes, Lee surrendered the other day too, and did he know any more live news? He acted kind of sore, but I heard somebody giggle, and that was when my real troubles started.

I looked toward the giggle expecting to see the kind of nurse they usually have, which, believe me, they're an awful thing for sick men to look at. I played football at college and I've been flying ever since, so I know my hospitals! But this girl looked like the nurses that other fellers who have been in the hospital are always telling you about. When you looked at her it was like when you've left the ground on a rainy day with everything dark and gray, and you fly up and up until suddenly you break through the clouds and you're all alone in a world where everything's blinding white and clean, cool blue. Anyway, that's how she looked when she smiled at me that day, and I smiled back and said "Hello, fair weather!" and then I passed out again. You see, one of those leg bones had come clear through.

Well, do you know who that girl was? That girl was Annabelle Green—*the* Annabelle Green—San Diego's Sweetheart, the Sunshine Girl, and all those other names. I guess today she's the most ballyhooed female since Cleopatra; but then she wasn't even a real nurse, but kind of a student that would get a nurse's license after she'd mechanicked in the hospital for a year or so.

Looking back at things now, I know Annabelle never intended to stick at nursing. She'd always lived in that hick town, and had been trying to get out since she was sixteen. She was so smart that she knew she wasn't the prettiest woman in the world, and when a pretty woman is that smart, she's a genius. The first few days I noticed that even the head doctor got fussed whenever he came within her wave length. And myself, I got to know her footstep coming down the hall, and I used to lie there listening for it and wishing they'd have somebody shave me so I wouldn't look like I'd just hit town on a freight. Annabelle's step was quick and busy and pretty and made you think of silk stockings and Spanish dancers. At first I thought it was only me that recognized it, but one day when I heard her coming, I saw the head doctor and the interne kind of prick up their ears and lay off dressing my leg and turn toward the door. She didn't come in, but just smiled as she twinkled past.

"Good morning, birdman!" she called.

"Good morning, sunrise!" I told her.

When I looked at the doctor and the interne, they were very busy and serious and fooling with the drain in my leg. And just then, somehow, all three of us were sore at each other and jealous, and we all knew why, though none of us had said a word.

Well, after I'd been a month in that bone garage, they took my leg out of the block and tackle that they'd rigged to the ceiling, and I could sit up and rest fairly comfortable. Annabelle would come in when she was off duty, and even sometimes when she wasn't; and we'd talk. She was ambitious, all right, and she admitted it. She wanted to *be* somebody and she'd give almost anything to get out of Caine. The trouble was, they'd always wanted her to give too much. For instance, there was a bird that could have made her Miss Caine in the Iowa State Beauty Contest, and if she hadn't drawn the line, it was a cinch she'd have been Miss America by the end of the season. Then she'd danced a hundred and seventeen hours without stopping in a Marathon contest, but all the publicity she got was a column in the local papers, and maybe half a stick in Chicago. It seemed that the guy who gave the prize got too eager.

Well, we talked about all this and about flying, and once in a while she'd swipe a medicine bottle full of alcohol, and we'd squeeze an orange and put in some ice and have a little snort, and we'd take turns on a cigarette so if we heard anybody coming she could pass it to me.

We got pretty chummy, all right, and in a nice kind of way. You see, I got to thinking a lot of her. My mother shipped my trunk out to me, and my scrap book of press notices was in it, and Annabelle read the ballyhoo and got all steamed up about it. And one day I showed her a post card I'd just got from Johnny Howe, who was flying the fairs down South with Diabolo, the wing walker. This Diabolo's a guy by the name of Haggerty, and he's an acrobat who climbs around on Johnny's ship and hangs from a trapeze on the landing gear and all that stuff, and the post card had a picture of them on it taken from another ship alongside them in the air.

"Oh," said Annabelle, "why, he's hanging by one hand! How high are they, Tommy?"

"Maybe a mile."

"Well, the height really don't make it any harder, does it?"

"No, but it don't make the falling any softer."

She acted like she didn't hear me. "My," she said, half to herself, "I bet there's a good living in that, isn't there?"

"Good while it lasts, but it's a long way down," and I lay thinking of the night out in Hollywood when we scraped up what was left of Ormer Locklear, the first man to walk a wing.

Annabelle laughed and suddenly stood up. "Look, you old mossback," she said, "I can do that stuff with the best of them!"

And she stepped to the foot of my bed, sprang up, grabbed the tackle on the ceiling they'd had my leg fastened to, and put on the neatest show of acrobatics I'd ever seen. It was big-time stuff and I mean it.

Well, she was still up there, and I guess I was blushing, because she wasn't exactly dressed for that kind of work, when in walked the head doctor. Annabelle did a double cut, dropped down to the bed, patted her nurse's cap straight, and smiled, "Good morning, Doctor!" Then she hopped to the floor, took a bow, fluttered out the door. And as the doc and I were staring toward where she'd vanished, we heard her giggle in the distance.

After a long, silent minute the doc turned and looked at me, and there was so much trouble in his face that I was sorry for him. He made a couple of false starts to say something, and finally walked over, shut the door, and coming back, sat down beside my bed.

"Son," he said, "there's no fool like an old fool—except a young one."

"Meaning you and me," I answered. "Thanks for the compliment."

"You're welcome. And now the old fool's going to come clean with the young one and—and—"

"Go ahead," I told him, "get it off your chest."

"Right," he said, bucking up and getting set, "I'm in love with Annabelle."

He sat there looking at me, ashamed, and sad, and at the same time proud as anything. And just then I realized that I liked him a lot, although until that moment I thought he was a washout. I didn't know what to say, so I just said: "Yes?"

"Yes!" he repeated, "I'm in love with Annabelle—and boy, how I've wanted to say it to somebody! Say it out loud, I mean. I'm in love with Annabelle. I haven't any business to be. I'm fifty-three years old. I'm married. My son's in college—"

"Well," I said, "what are you telling it all to me for?"

"I don't know, except I'd like to help her—and you. I see she's wearing your fraternity pin. Have you come to any understanding yet? I mean, do you know what you're going to do?"

When he asked me this, I lay back and thought for a minute, and suddenly I began to realize that he was a pretty wise old boy at that. "No," I said kind of slow, "Annabelle and I haven't come to any agreement—and yet, I guess I can see what's going to happen all right."

"What?"

"Well, now that you speak of it, it all seems pretty clear that she and I are going on the road, flying exhibitions, and she is going to do aërial acrobatics and wing walking. She hasn't said so, but I guess she's kind of made up her mind."

"I know!" he said. "Oh, don't I know! It was the same way when she came to me with a blister on her heel after some fool dancing contest she was in. She made up her mind she wanted to be a nurse; she didn't have to say anything, I just knew it. And so—she became a nurse. The poor chap who owned the theater sold out, lost half his wad, and went God knows where. And before him was Finley, who owned the newspaper—"

"Oh, yes, she's told me about those guys," I said, acting as tough as my game leg would let me. "Are you just another one of that kind?"

"No," he bristled, "I'm not that kind, and neither were they. I know what you mean, and I knew Edward Shanley and George Finley as well as I know myself. They were on the level with Annabelle and don't you forget it. They, too, were—well, *old fools*. Why, son," his voice dropped, "here am I, fifty-three years old. Too old for her by thirty years. I love my wife—sure, I love my wife—but gosh, what thoughts I've had! South America—Australia—I've thought of them all. And do you know, I've spent hours in front of the mirror wondering if I could put a stitch or so in the skin on my temples, under the hair, to pull up my face and get the wrinkles out? Imagine *me* thinking of that! I'm crazy as a loon, hey? Crazy!

"Well," he stood up, all very brisk, his voice cold again, "so Miss Green is going to do wing walking, is she?"

"She is," I reassured him as confidently as I could.

"Do you want her to do it?"

It was my turn to be uncomfortable. "No," I said, "I don't. Wing walking's bad enough even with yeggs like Diabolo, which you don't care whether they fall off or not. But with Annabelle to worry about—well, Doctor, it'll be hell." And I guess I squirmed a little when I said it.

"Son," he said, "I'm going away on my vacation tonight. I've made a good job of your leg, and in three weeks you'll be out of here. So will Annabelle. Tommy," he took my hand, "be careful of her—"

That was the last I saw of him, and in a month Annabelle and I were in Florida. I had to go to see the aunt she'd lived with in Caine; she was an old crab, and so was her other aunt who lived in Miami.

I had twelve thousand dollars which had been my take on the season before I crashed, and Elmer Baker gave me a nice new ship on time payments. Annabelle and I flew every morning working up our act. And I want to say there never was a girl like Annabelle. Maybe you've done night flying on the air mail, or got shot at by Richtofen during the war, but I bet you wouldn't do half the stuff that Annabelle did after two weeks in the air.

Every night I'd wake up two or three times with my heart stopped dead, dreaming of her falling. Sometimes, 'way up there in the blue above Biscayne Bay it used to make me weak and sick to see her walking out there on the wing, leaning against the wind, hanging by one hand over six thousand feet of nothing and throwing kisses at me with the other. And we'd end up the act by going into a spin and her jumping out with her parachute; only she'd keep the chute closed and drop like a rock until she was six or seven hundred feet from the ground. Then she'd pull the ring, the chute would burst open like a big white flower, and she'd float down and land.

This business of keeping the chute closed was her own idea, and gosh, it was awful. "There's a kick in it, big boy!" she'd say. "With that speed, the old air sure hugs your Annabelle tight. It's—it's wonderful! Bet you're jealous, big boy!"

"Maybe so, but don't do it," I'd plead with her. "Some time when you're going headfirst and sideways, you'll get dizzy and forget to pull that ring." You see, she'd be falling at around four hundred miles an hour, and that's faster than thoughts can travel through nerves. It was terrible, all right, but it sure got the crowds.

Yes, we got plenty of crowds. When we left Florida we had solid booking right across the country to California, and we packed 'em into the fair grounds all the way. Our act was a knockout, and Annabelle was in heaven, by which I mean she was on the front page.

As for me, well, I guess I'm too professional. What I mean is, when I'm working, I'm working. I never stopped loving Annabelle, but as long as we were working, I figured I couldn't say anything about it. I just keep thinking and dreaming and worrying about her, and wishing the season would end so I could ask her to marry me. Somehow I had a hunch that if I asked her then, I'd lose my nerve and we'd both get killed. Or her anyway, which would be worse. So I just said nothing, and kept on flying and watching her and worrying. And even in the evenings at the hotel I didn't stick around her much, but would leave her with the fair committee or the newspaper people or the ladies' club, and go by myself for a walk or to the movies.

When we got to San Diego we met George Massy. In fact, it was him who booked us to fly. He owns about everything in sight out there, and he's worth a sock of money. From what I saw of him he didn't seem to be a bad skate, either. Kind of quiet and serious and a real nice guy. And it was him who backed us to fly the Atlantic. Annabelle talked him into it.

Now don't make any mistake about my ever wanting to fly the Atlantic. To me the Atlantic was just so much water to get drowned in. Old terra firma was always good enough for me. I wasn't out to kid anybody about blazing the way for science, or carrying good will to the heathen Frenchmen, or any of that stuff. I knew what an aëroplane could do, and I figured if we made it, Annabelle and I'd be lucky and famous and—which was most important—married.

But Annabelle was rarin' to go, and as long as she wanted to, it was all right with me. So we came East, and while she was having her picture taken thirty times a day, and was endorsing cigarettes and face creams, I was out on Long Island working with Charlie Kirk in his shop, getting the special plane ready. I didn't see much of her, but of course I read every day in the papers about the Sunshine Girl going to fly to France for her Paris gowns, and sometimes there'd be a note about her co-pilot, which meant me.

Well, eight weeks before we were set to go, Massy sailed for France to work up the ballyhoo over there. Meanwhile, you know how the papers played it up on this side. And one foggy morning, which seems like a thousand years ago, I dragged the ship over the trees and the movie cameras, took a long easy turn over Mineola, and headed for the ocean.

It may sound funny to you, but I really don't remember much about that flight. I was in a daze. My nerves were working and I flew because it's always been instinct with me to fly, but my mind was sort of a blank. I was scared, scared all the way; I won't try to kid you that I wasn't scared, because I was. And I had been for months. Worrying, worrying all the time. And toward the last I'd been posing for pictures and answering fool questions all

WHERE ALL GOOD FLAPPERS GO

day, and lying awake all night. I wouldn't go through it again for a million dollars.

There's only one thing I really do remember. That was the cigarette smoke in the plane. You see, we had a cabin ship, and if you opened the portholes it got too cold, and so we had to leave them closed. This would have been O.K. if Annabelle hadn't smoked all the time. I asked her not to, but she only laughed and patted my cheek. The air in there was fierce and I had a blind headache, but she wanted to smoke, so that was that. She spent her time between sleeping and smoking. I spent all the time looking at sixteen different instruments, listening to the motor, looking out for ships, worrying, and having a headache.

But anyway, I found France. Found it within ten miles of the spot I was aiming for. And when I pointed to the Cap Duthiez lighthouse, winking down there in the gloom, and shouted, *"Paris in seventy minutes,"* what do you suppose Annabelle did? Kiss me? No, sir! She took her flashlight, shined it on her face with one hand, and fixed her make-up with the other.

Well, you read all about our landing—how fifty million Frenchmen, or whatever it was, came out on the field and shed tears and shouted about Lafayette. And when I finally unjointed myself and they lugged me out, the reception committee was leading Annabelle off.

"But don't you want your baggage, Miss Green?" asked one of them.

"I've only a suitcase," she answered, and then pointing at me, "My mechanic will look after it."

And—well, now you know how Annabelle Green flew the Atlantic.

Next day, or maybe the day after, I met Massy in the Ritz Bar. At least I guess it was the Ritz Bar.

"Oh, hello," he said, kind of embarrassed, "how are you today?"

"I'm fine, how are you?"

"Great," he said. "Are you all rested up?"

"Rested—and liquored," I told him. "How are you feeling?"

"I told you before I felt all right," he said. "Say, what's on your chest?"

"Nothing," I answered. "Only I wanted to ask you a question."

"Shoot," he said, looking at his watch.

"Well," I began, picking up my glass, "you know who I am, don't you?"

"Why, of course I do, Tommy. What do you ask such a question for?"

"Oh, I was just wondering. But did you ever hear of Edward Shanley, who owned the theater in Caine, Iowa?"

"Why, no."

"Or of George Finley, newspaper publisher of the same place?"

He shook his head.

"Or of Doctor Casper Ricker, of the Caine Memorial Hospital?"

"Nope, I never did."

"Well, you ought to," I said. And then I guess I passed out cold.

MONKEY JUNK

Zora Neale Hurston

Pittsburgh Courier, March 5th 1927

1. And it came to pass in those days that one dwelt in the land of the Harlemites who thought that he knew all the law and the prophets.

2. Also when he arose in the morning and at noonday his mouth flew open and he said, "Verily, I am a wise guy. I knoweth all about women."

3. And in the cool of the evening he saith and uttereth, "I know all that there is about the females. Verily, I shall not let myself be married."

4. Thus he counselled within his liver for he was persuaded that merry maidens were like unto death for love of him.

5. But none desired him.

6. And in that same year a maiden gazeth upon his checkbook and she coveted it.

7. Then became she coy and sweet with flattery and he swalloweth the bait.

8. And in that same month they became man and wife.

9. Then did he make a joyful noise saying, "Behold, I have chosen a wife, yea verily a maiden I have exalted above all others, for see I have wed her."

10. And he gave praises loudly unto the Lord saying, "I thank thee that I am not as other men—stupid and blind and imposed upon by every female that listeth. Behold how diligently I have sought and winnowed out the chaff from the wheat! Verily have I chosen well, and she shalt be rewarded for her virtue, for I shall approve and honor her."

11. And for an year did he wooed her with his shekels and comfort her with his checkbook and she endured him.

12. Then did his hand grow weary of check signing and he slackened his speed.

13. Then did his pearl of great price form the acquaintance of many men and they prospered her.

14. Then did he wax wrathful in his heart because other men posed the tongue into the cheek and snickered behind the hand as he passed, saying, "Verily his head is decorated with the horns, he that is so wise and knoweth all the law and the profits."

16. And he chided his wife saying, "How now dost thou let others less worthy bite thy husband in the back? Verily now I am sore and I meaneth not maybe."

17. But she answered him laughingly saying, "Speak not out of turn. Thou wast made to sign checks, not to make love signs. Go now, and broil thyself an radish."

18. Then answered he, "Thy tongue doth drip sassiness and thy tonsils impudence, know ye not that I shall leave thee?"

19. But she answered him with much gall, "Thou canst not do better than to go—but see that thou leave behind thee many signed checks."

20. And when he heard these things did he gnash his teeth and sweat great hunks of sweat.

21. And he answered, "Verily I am through with thee—thou canst NOT snore in my ear no more."

22. Then placeth she her hands upon the hips and sayeth, "Let not that lie get out, for thou art NOT through with me."

23. And he answered her saying, "Thou hast flirted copiously and surely the back-biters shall sign thy checks henceforth—for I am through with thee."

24. But she answered him, "Nay, thou art not through with me—for I am a darned sweet woman and thou knowest it. Don't let that lie get out. Thou shalt never be through with me as long as thou hath bucks."

25. "Thou are very dumb for now that I, thy husband, knoweth that thou art a flirt, making glad the heart of back-biters, I shall support thee no more—for verily know I ALL the law and the profits thereof."

26. Then answered she with a great sassiness of tongue, "Neither shalt not deny me thy shekels for I shall seek them in law, yea shall I lift up my voice and the lawyers and judges shall hear my plea and thou shalt pay dearly. For, verily, they permit no turpitudinous mama to suffer. Selah and amen."

27. But he laughed at her saying hey! hey! hey! many times for verily he considered with his kidneys that he knew his rights.

28. Then went she forth to the market place and sought the places that deal in fine raiment and bought much fine linen, yea lingerie and hosiery of fine silk, for she knew in her heart that she must sit in the seat of a witness and hear testimony to many things lest she get no alimony.

29. Even of French garters bought she the finest.

30. Then hastened she away to the houses where sat pharisees and Sadducees and those who know the law and the profits, and one among them was named Miles Paige, him being a young man of a fair countenance.

31. And she wore her fine raiment and wept mightily as she told of her wrongs.

32. But he said unto her, "Thou has not much of a case, but I shall try it for thee. But practice not upon me neither with tears nor with hosiery—for verily I be not a doty juryman. Save thy raiment for the courts."

33. But her husband sought no counsel for he said, "Surely she hath sinned against me—even cheated most

vehemently. Shall not the court rebuke her when I shall tell of it. For verily I know also the law."

34. Then came the officer of the court and said, "Thou shalt give thy wife temporary alimony of fifty shekels until the trial cometh."

35. And he was wrathful but he wagged the head and said, "I pay now, but after the trial I shall pay no more. He that laughest last is worth two in the bush."

36. And entered he boldly into the courts of law and sat down at the trial. And his wife and her lawyer came also.

37. But he looked upon the young man and laughed for Miles Paige had yet no beard and the husband looked upon him with scorn, even as Goliath looked upon David.

38. And the judge sat upon the high seat and the jury sat in the box and many came to see and to hear, and the husband rejoiced within his heart for the multitude would hear him speak and confound the learned doctors.

39. Then called he witnesses and they did testify that the wife was an flirt. And they sat upon the stand again

and the young pharisee, even Paige questioned them, and verily they were steadfast.

40. Then did the husband rejoice exceedingly and ascended the stand and testified of his great goodness unto his spouse.

41. And when the young lawyer asked no questions he waxed stiff necked for he divined that he was afraid.

42. And the young man led the wife upon the stand and she sat upon the chair of witnesses and bear testimony.

43. And she gladdened the eyes of the jury and the judge leaned down from his high seat and beamed upon her for verily she was some brown.

44. And she turned soulful eyes about her and all men yearned to fight for her.

45. Then did she testify and cross the knees, even the silk covered joints, and weep. For verily she spoke of great evils visited upon her.

46. And the young pharisee questioned her gently and the jury leaneth forward to catch every word which fell from her lips.

47. For verily her lips were worth it.

48. Then did they all glare upon the husband; yea, the judge and jury frowned upon the wretch, and would have choked him.

49. And when the testimony was finished and she had descended from the stand, did the young man, even Miles Paige stand before the jury and exhort them.

50. Saying, "When in the course of human events, Romeo, Romeo, wherefore art thou and how come what for?" And many other sayings of exceeding wiseness.

51. Then began the jury to foam at the mouth and went the judge into centrance. Moreover made the lawyer many gestures which confounded the multitude, and many cried, "Amen" to his sayings.

52. And when he had left off speaking then did the jury cry out "Alimony (which being interpreted means all his jack) aplenty!"

53. And the judge was pleased and said, "An hundred shekels per month."

54. Moreover did he fine the husband heavily for his cruelties and abuses and his witnesses for perjury.

55. Then did the multitude rejoice and say "Great is Miles Paige, and mighty is the judge and jury."

56. And then did the husband rend his garments and cover his head with ashes for he was undone.

57. But privately he went to her and said, "Surely, thou hast tricked me and I am undone by thy guile. Wherefore, now should I not smite thee, even mash thee in the mouth with my fist?"

58. And she answered him haughtily saying, "Did I not say that thou wast a dumb cluck? Go to, now, thou had better not touch this good brown skin."

59. And he full of anger spoke unto her, "But I shall surely smite thee in the nose—how doth old heavy hitting papa talk?"

60. And she made answer unto him, "Thou shalt surely go to the cooler if thou stick thy rusty fist in my face, for I shall holler like a pretty white woman."

61. And he desisted. And after many days did he receive a letter saying, "Go to the monkeys, thou hunk of mud, and learn things and be wise."

62. And he returned unto Alabama to pick cotton.

Selah.

WHY GIRLS GO SOUTH

Anita Loos

Harper's Bazaar, January 1926

S OCIETY NOTE: "Among those who are now flitting Florida-wise is the gorgeous Judith Revell, in this instance accompanied by her aristocratic mother, her father, and her maiden Aunt Mary. Judy always manages to keep well to the fore in the public prints, and the Florida season is sure to be considerably *égayé* by her presence, because where Judy is, there is always action of one kind or another.

"The migration of the Revell clan adds two of the oldest Knickerbocker names to the Florida roster, which to date, perhaps, has been made up of a too generous a sprinkling of the *nouveaux riches*. But, with the Revells, goes not only the substantial cognomen of Revell *père*, but the much-to-be-conjured-with name of van Tassell, to which Judy's mother was born, and which now is carried by her maiden aunt, Miss Mary van Tassell. If one wanted to write a modern fairy-story, it would seem that one could not imagine a more glamorous heroine than the lovely Judy actually is in real life—truly, 'a girl who has everything.' To be nineteen, outstandingly beautiful, talented, and with a magnificent social background, what more has life to offer? Judy's career is going to bear watching."

If Judy's career is going to bear watching, we may as well begin at the beginning of it and let the reader in on a scene that took place one morning last December.

The setting is the red and gold salon of the old Revell home in the once ultra-aristocratic Murray Hill district of New York. The atmosphere breathes long-standing tradition, and elegance which has stood a little too long.

On a Louis Quinze table rests the famous silver-gilt urn, which was presented by the late Czar Nicholas of Russia to the present head of the house of Revell, when he was American Consul General in St. Petersburg. Inside the urn is a dun for repairs on the roof of the house, due since a year ago August. To the left of the table hangs a portrait of Julian Revell the First, founder of the family, self-made millionaire, and head of the New York Anti-vice league that cleaned Manhattan of sin in 1871, and gave it the push that sent it headlong into its present state of grace. On a gilt console table, underneath this portrait, rests a current copy of the *Daily Views*, with a two-column picture of the present daughter of the house,

Miss Judith Revell, doing the Charleston at a lawn fête in Southampton; her underwear, a one-piece step-in, is seen to be edged with exquisite old point d'Alencon. Against the opposite wall stands a Louis Quinze spinet, on top of which is an ormolu jewel box, presented to Judith's mother, Emma, on the occasion of her marriage, by the late Ward McAllister. It contains three soiled aspirin tablets, an autographed photograph of the Grand Duchess Kyril, and a notice to the effect that Emma has been posted at the Colony Club.

It is a high moment in the Revell salon, and the air is tense with dramatic feeling. Those present are:

Ex-Consul General, Julian Revell. The last time he was sober was just before his graduation from Harvard in 1886, and he can remember nearly everything prior to that date, but his mind is a bit hazy as to what has occurred since. He made a record as Consul General in St. Petersburg by investing a fortune in the off-stage activities of the members of the Imperial Ballet, went seriously into the drinking of vodka, and won the non-stop handicap away from a certain Grand Duke who had been trained from birth for the championship, thus carrying the American flag right through to the top. He now leads a regular life, automatically making the Racquet Club by four o'clock every afternoon, but if he ever learns about prohibition, it is going to go hard with him.

Mrs. Revell, born van Tassell. Emma van Tassell was a great catch for Julian in 1889, a van Tasell being of the finest old Dutch stock, and much too good for a Revell. In fact, it was this match that opened up the last social gates to the Revell clan. Emma, at the present time, is fairly clean without being tidy. In the old days, she possessed a maid who had a genius for being able to keep her stockings from bagging at the ankles, but the maid went the way of other lost luxuries. Emma is wearing a vintage gown of the House of Paquin, with a real lace bertha, and she thinks she is wearing Revell pearls, not knowing that Julian had them replaced by "Indetectibles" the time he was caught with a blonde in a badger game in Atlantic City.

A third member, and the most important of the Revell conference, is Judith Revell, called Judy, the flower of this fine old stock—beautiful with a beauty that comes only through breeding. It is a matter of social record that when she made her entrance at the famous Cosden ball, given on Long Island in honor of the Prince of Wales, those who stood near His Royal Highness overheard the Prince exclaim, "Hot Dog!" Judy wears an exquisitely simple black Chanel frock for which she owes Vendel $195.00, making her bill to date, $3,434.50.

The fourth and last member of this quaint quartette is Emma's sister, Aunt Mary van Tassell, who is wearing a white shirt-waist and a black and white pepper-and-salt skirt. Aunt Mary, having always had a mind of her own, never seemed to need masculine companionship, and has reached the age of fifty-two, unmarried. As she says of herself, "Up to the age of eighteen I was called a tomboy— after eighteen I became an old maid and, in my day, that was all there was to it. But, if I had been born in this generation, my dear, I should be clipping my hair, dressing like a man from the waist up, and leading a life that only Havelock Ellis could explain." She has had a peculiar history. Twenty-five years ago she deserted New York society because she found it dull, and went to Europe, where she made the rounds of continental pensions for nearly a quarter of a century.

Returning to America only three months ago, she found conditions that amazed and delighted her. Social life, when she was a girl, had meant a succession of polite and respectable gaieties that had bored her stiff. Today, she finds everything changed for the better. To put it in Aunt Mary's own words: "Why, when I was a young thing, men used to get squiffy only at their clubs or at stag parties. We girls never saw any of the fun. *Now* I find you all getting tight together, right in your own salons, and no end of amusement! And twenty-five years ago, if a man so much as kissed a girl without proposing honorable matrimony, her father and brothers came to the rescue and arranged a military wedding, at the point of a gun. As a result, scandals were scarce and life was anemic. But today I find that even the classic excuse for a military wedding isn't taken so seriously. How amusing!

"And, in my time, people had to stick to their kind and be bored to tears. I can remember how we girls used to hear vague rumors about the matrimonial career of Lillian Russell, and if we were very, very good, Mamma took us to a New Year's matinée, and let me look at her across the footlights. What nonsense!

"Today, a deb can go up to the Colony restaurant, have luncheon with Texas Guinon, and get full details of all the fun, first hand. Delightful!"

And so, after twenty-five years of retirement, Aunt Mary has decided to re-enter American Society. Aunt Mary's attitude, however, is not shared by Emma, who still sticks to the old traditions. It was Emma who had organized this morning's session, the subject under discussion being:

First: That last night Judy was out again till morning.

Second: That having left the house to attend the Henry Abel-Abels' dinner to the Dowager Duchess of Dexter, she did not return until 11 a.m. next day, her evening gown covered by the raincoat of the hat-check girl at the Hotel Astor.

Third: Emma, feeling that this was a bit thick, had gone through Judy's effects and found in her vanity case a check for two thousand dollars, made out to her daughter, and signed by the name of a strange man.

"Who is this Herman Gluckman, and why is he giving you two thousand dollars?" demands Emma.

"Yes, why did he do it, and what's his address?" speaks up the ex-Consul General.

Judy overlooks her father's query, which passes unnoticed, as Father's brain seldom retains long enough to follow up a comeback.

"I can't wait to learn, after all that you girls hand out for nothing, what there is left worth two thousand dollars," says Aunt Mary.

Emma now breaks into tears and turns to her husband.

"Julian," she says, "Julian, do something! Try to realize that your daughter's good name has probably gone beyond recall!"

"Just so," says Julian, and turning to Judy he speaks.

"To think that you, my daughter, should so far forget her fair name as to—as to—as to—"

"Yes, Father, go on."

"What was I talking about?"

"Apple sauce," says Aunt Mary.

"Exactly—best apples in the world—right on the old van Tassell place in Rhinebeck—best hard cider in the—that reminds me—I'm due at the club."

"Sit down, Julian!" says Emma. "We are going to have the truth about last night's business before one of us leaves this room!"

*

Judy draws herself up to her full height.

"Well—since last night was a turning point in my life," she says, "perhaps it is just as well that you all learn something about it!"

"Go ahead," says Aunt Mary, "but you can't make me believe that Herman got his money's worth."

Judy withers Aunt Mary.

"None of you understands me! I loathe and hate our whole existence! I want to be out in the world among people who do things—but of course you've never seemed to realize that I have a temperament."

"How did you find that out?" asks Aunt Mary.

"It's obvious to any one who really knows me. Why I go perfectly mad every time I hear jazz! Every boy I've ever danced with has said that I am *full* of temperament!"

"Oh, dear, what is she talking about?" asks Emma.

"You had the same thing when you were a girl," says Aunt Mary, "only in those days we called by its right name and the man had to marry you."

Judy overlooks her aunt completely.

"Temperament, Mother, is what makes people artists."

"Just as often as liquor makes people Edgar Allan Poe," says Aunt Mary.

"What's that? Liquor?" speaks up Julian. "Make mine Scotch."

"Well," says Aunt Mary, "all of these dancing boys say that you are full of temperament—now where does that lead us?"

"What it all means is, that I have simply got to express myself. But, of course, you can't understand! I never expected to get any encouragement from the family—I had to go to outsiders for understanding and sympathy!"

"'Outsiders' meaning Herman Glickman, I take it," says Aunt Mary.

"Wherever did you meet a person with a name like that?" asks Emma.

"Mr. Glickman knows Eddie Goldmark, and Eddie introduced me."

Emma all but faints.

"And who might Eddie be, if anything?" asks Aunt Mary.

"Mr. Goldmark is the famous motion-picture magnate," answers Judy.

"Judy," demands her mother, "who dared introduce you to a motion-picture magnate?"

"The Duchess of Dexter."

"And how, may I ask, did this motion-picture person meet the Duchess of Dexter?"

"The Queen of Ruritania introduced her to him in London, and when she came over here, of course she looked him up—"

"Don't tell me that this motion-picture person was at the Abels' dinner to the Duchess last night!" says Emma.

"He was not! If he had been, we might have stuck it to the finish."

"Do you mean to say that you left the Abels' dinner before it was over?"

"Mother dear, that dinner was ghastly! We left before the coffee."

"You walked out of the Abels' dinner to the Duchess! With *whom*, may I ask?"

"With the Duchess."

"What?"

"Mother dear, if you want to hear the Duchess's own words—"

"Oh yes! Let's hear the Duchess's own words," says Aunt Mary. "She learned some good ones from the late King Edward when she was a girl."

"The Duchess said, 'If I don't get out of this house soon, I'll be all over itch!'"

"Best thing for an itch," speaks up Julian, "is a rub with pure grain alcohol—get it in a drug store on Third Avenue—don't even need a prescription—purest alcohol in the world—can put it right in your stomach!"

"And where, may I ask, did you and the Duchess go when you left the Abels'?" inquired Emma.

"We went to a party that Mr. Goldmark was giving to Mr. Allister Wardley."

"Not the Allister Wardleys of Philadelphia?" asks Emma.

"Of course!"

"And what is an Allister Wardley doing with a-a-a-Goldmark?" gasps Emma.

"She took him away from the Countess of Menander," answers Judy.

Emma staggers to a chair.

"I am stronger than you, Emma," says Aunt Mary, "let me go on with this," and turning to Judy she asks what happened next.

"Well, I met Mr. Goldmark, and danced with him, and he told me that I would register 100 S.A. in Hollywood."

"Yes? And what is '100 S.A.'?"

"S.A. stands for sex appeal, and 100 is the highest they can give you, even in Hollywood—and you know what a compliment Mr. Goldmark paid me, when he only gives Lowell Sherman 75."

Emma wants to know if the above-mentioned gentleman is a connection of the Lowells of Massachusetts and the Shermans of Georgia.

"Mother dear, if you knew anything at all about drama," says Judy, "you would know that Lowell Sherman is a perfectly divine actor, and when he played Casanova, seven girls were expelled from Miss Blakeley's."

Emma, knowing nothing of drama, is silenced.

"Well—Mr. Goldmark said that it would be a crime for me not to have career—and he said that if I could come down to Florida next month, he could give me a part in a movie, but you know how much chance there is for me to get to Florida, where one has to pay bills, unless one goes on a grand scale, which I can't."

"I thought these movie queens were highly paid persons," says Aunt Mary.

Julian awakes with a jerk.

"Movie queens?" he exclaims. "Bring 'em in!"

"They are highly paid after they get started," answers Judy, "and this would be my start. Believe me, Aunt Mary, it's a great opportunity. Just think, I would get twenty-five dollars every day I worked!"

"And how often would you work?"

"Well, Mr. Goldmark says at least one day a week."

"Judy, you are not only chuck-full of S.A. but you're a financial genius besides!"

"I don't understand it at all," says Emma, "but it sounds like Bolshevism."

"Speaking of Russia," says Julian, "best vodka in the world—right over on Fifty-third Street! Sixty dollars a case! Grand Duke Alexis has more customers than he can supply."

Judy yawns and looks at her wrist watch, which so far has been a total loss to the firm of Cartier.

"I've an engagement at one-thirty," she says, "so you'll please make this inquisition as short as possible."

"You're not going to step out of this house," says Emma, "without taking your aunt or myself along."

"Mother, don't be stupid!" says Judy. "The first place I'm going is to the Joshua Aldersons' luncheon for Bishop

Small, and heaven knows nothing could possibly happen to me there!"

Emma cocks an eye at her daughter.

"Judy," she says, "now I know you are lying to me! I know very well that not even wild horses could drag you to old lady Alderson's!"

"Mother," answers Judy, "you don't seem to realize that last night was a turning point in my life. From now on, I am going to accept every stupid, exclusive invitation that comes my way."

"What's all this?" asks Aunt Mary.

"It's perfectly simple," says Judy. "This morning I went to see one of the brainiest publicity women in New York, Miss Steinbach. I told her that I was going in for an artistic career and asked if she would undertake my publicity and she said that on one condition, and that was I give her something to work on. Because, you see, the only talking point she has on me is a purely social one. So she said that I would have to change my mode of life and go to the exclusive parties now and then, so as to give her something to get her teeth into. Because she also handles other artists—Ann Pennington, for instance—and she says that as matters stand now she doesn't see much difference between my career and Ann Pennington's, except that Ann Pennington knows how to dance."

*

Emma is too dazed to come out of this tangle of cross-thought without help. So Aunt Mary jumps into the breach.

"Well, Emma," she says, "half the women in society are going in for the—mm—Arts, and as far as I'm concerned, I'm all for it! It makes the world a brighter and funnier place to live in. What if a career *is* only an alibi for being rowdy? At least, it's better than being rowdy without one. And, as I take it, this Steinbach woman is the only person capable of keeping Judy in respectable company for even a small portion of the day. Put your brains to work, Emma, and give it some thought!"

"Oh, dear," says Emma, "I don't know what to think—after all that happened to Judy last night—"

"Well, buck up, Emma," says Aunt Mary, "we haven't yet heard *all* that happened, and it may get worse." Then turning to Judy, she continues, "you have accounted successfully for about half the night. What happened next? I'm dying to know!"

"Well—Mr. Goldmark and Mrs. Allister Wardley and the Duchess and two gentlemen and I—"

"Do I know the two gentlemen?" asks Emma, hoping against hope that they may be in the Social Register.

"They were Damon Giles and Spottiswood Irving," says Judy. "They are interior decorators, and the Duchess adores them!"

"Yes, I know," says Aunt Mary. "When she's out with the two of them together, she feels she has a man about."

"They are artists, Aunt Mary!"

"Ah, yes—I always forget that we are moving in the realm of Art!"

"Well—the six of us went up to the Love Nest."

"Whose love nest!" asks Julian.

"The Love Nest is a divine cabaret in Forty-Eight Street. Well, by seven o'clock, Mr. Goldmark and I were left alone and we had a long, serious talk."

"What happened to the other Art lovers?" asks Aunt Mary.

"Aunt Mary, have you got to know every insignificant thing that happened last night?" asks Judy.

"If anything happened last night that *was* insignificant, go on and tell your mother. It might cheer her up."

"Well, while Mr. Goldmark was out getting more Scotch—"

"Yes—yes—" speaks up Julian.

"A waiter was rude to Spottiswood—"

"And what did the waiter do to Spottiswood?"

"Well, you see, Spottiswood told the waiter to remove an electric candelabra, because he is very sensitive to light effects and he considered that the Duchess was badly lit."

"Lit!" exclaims Julian. "Good for her!"

"So then the waiter refused and he called Spottiswood a name."

"What name?"

"Well, a name that means a man—who is an interior decorator."

"Oh, dear," says Emma, "I don't know what you're talking about—do we have to go into all this detail?"

"I wouldn't miss a word of it for money," says Aunt Mary. "And what did Spottiswood do then?"

"Well, Aunt Mary," says Judy, "he got into an argument with the waiter, and if you have got to know every single word of it, I'll try to remember."

"Go ahead," says Aunt Mary, "And don't hold out on me!"

"Well—Spottiswood was very dignified, but he told the waiter that if he knew anything at all about history, he would realize that every great man who ever lived was an interior decorator at heart."

"What?" asks Aunt Mary.

"Spottiswood knows what he is talking about, because he has gone into the subject thoroughly, and he said that when he visited Stratford-on-Avon, he proved to himself that Shakespeare may have spent his spare time writing drama, but it was not for nothing that his house looked like a high-class shop on the Boston Post Road."

"Yes, yes, go on!"

"Well, he also said that one trip to Mount Vernon had convinced him that winning a few battles didn't interfere with George Washington being able to put the right rag rug where it was needed. And as far as Napoleon was concerned, any one who had ever been to Malmaison could see at a glance that he knew where to put a dash of

Empire blue to get the effect he was looking for. And then the waiter got rude."

"Oh, goody! And what did the waiter do?"

"Well, he called to one of the other waiters and said, 'Come on over and look at what just said that George Washington embroidered the Constitution on a tea cosy.'"

"Delightful! And what happened then?"

"Well, the Duchess was furious and sent for the proprietor, who was perfectly charming about it all, but he couldn't do anything, because the waiter was the personal representative of the prohibition officer in that District, so he suggested that as long as Spottiswood and Damon got on the waiter's nerves, we had better go to another place. So the two boys and the Duchess went on to Childs, but Isabel Wardley and I had to wait for Mr. Goldmark to come back."

"And did he bring the Scotch?" asks Julian.

Every once in a while Julian astounds his family by a real feat of memory.

"Well," says Judy, "it finally got late, so we started away, but as we were going out Isabel fell upstairs and strained her scar—"

"Her what?"

"She had her face lifted two weeks ago, and it isn't healed yet. So we had to take her home to put ice on it, and then Mr. Goldmark and I went to the Astor Hotel for breakfast, and I accepted his offer to work in the movies, but I told him that I would simply have to have money to get to Florida—and he suggested Mr. Glickman."

"Why didn't this Goldmark person offer to be your banker, since he is rich, and you are so full of S.A.?" asks Aunt Mary.

"Mr. Goldmark said that he would be glad to finance my career, but he is crazy about Isabel Wardley, and she is violently jealous, so he wouldn't dare. And the next best thing was Mr. Glickman."

Emma looks faint.

"If you want to leave the room for the remainder of this, Emma," says Aunt Mary, "I'll get the story myself and break it to you a little at a time."

"No," says Emma, "my great-great-grandmother carried water to the Continentals on Morristown Heights! I can stand it."

"Then go on, Judy," says Aunt Mary.

"Well, after breakfast, Mr. Goldmark said that the one person who could arrange matters with Herman Glickman was a lady who lives on West End Avenue so we—"

"Wait a moment—wait a moment," says Aunt Mary, "even my old brain is beginning to weaken! What did you say this lady was?"

"She is the lady who gets girls in touch with Herman Glickman."

"What's her address?" speaks up Julian.

"But what—" breaks in Emma.

"Emma," says Aunt Mary, "if you had the faintest idea of what is being discussed here, I'd order you from the room."

"I'm just as unhappy when I don't understand," says Emma.

"Well, Judy, what happened then?"

"We started to West End Avenue to see—this lady, and as we were leaving the Astor, the hat-check girl, who is a friend of Mr. Goldmark's, noticed that I was in evening dress and lent me her coat."

"The hat-check girl noticed this? And where were your own powers of observation?"

"Our minds were on other things."

"That's right," says Aunt Mary, "I always forget that your minds are on Art."

"Well, we picked up this lady at her house and came back to Mr. Glickman's place—and then Mr. Goldmark had to leave us. So the lady introduced me to Mr. Glickman, and he was perfectly delightful, and in less than ten minutes I agreed to his proposition for two thousand dollars."

"Well," says Aunt Mary, "we may just as well brace ourselves for the worst. What was the proposition?"

"I hate to tell you, because you'll make a furious fuss, and it really isn't anything at all."

"No—in these days, I notice it isn't," says Aunt Mary.

"Well, all I had to do was sign a paper for Mr. Glickman allowing him to use my name and pedigree and photograph in some very high-class advertisements that go only in the best magazines, together with a statement that I have been cured of seborrhea."

"What's—seborrhea?" asks Julian.

"You'll never know," answers Aunt Mary, "because I've read those advertisements and they say that only a mother would tell you."

The discussion gets no further, because Emma has fainted and it takes some time to bring her to. As she regains consciousness, she murmurs instructions to Judy to remember her ancestry, particularly on her mother's side, and finally picks up enough strength to rise to her feet, order Judy to tear up the check, lock herself in her room and spend the remainder of her life in prayer.

"I knew exactly what would happen if I told you," says Judy, "and I'm not going to stay here to be insulted by petty minds!"

"No," says Aunt Mary, "why should you, when all the high-class magazines in America will soon be on the job?"

Judy turns to Aunt Mary.

"I must say, I'm surprised at you, Aunt Mary," she says, "I thought that *you* would understand."

Aunt Mary thinks a moment, right through the sobs of Emma and the snores of Julian.

"As a matter of fact, Emma," she says, "I do think that you are taking this a bit too seriously."

"Mary," asks Emma, "how could it be worse?"

"Easily," answers Judy, "the advertisement says in plain English that I've been *cured* of seborrhea! Suppose I had to say I have it yet!"

"Exactly," says Aunt Mary. "I'm beginning to be won around."

"And think of the publicity if gives me when I'm starting on a career!"

"Publicity!" gasps Emma. "Publicity! To think that we—!"

"Oh, Mother," cries Judy, "it isn't as though I were the only one who ever did this! How do you suppose the Duchess of Dexter got the money to come to America? The only income she has in the world is rent on her flat in London."

"She can't get much for that," speaks up Aunt Mary, "because the view looks smack on the Albert Memorial."

"Of course!" says Judy. "The Duchess signed up for seven thousand dollars. It's frightfully simple. Everybody's doing it."

"But Judy," asks Aunt Mary, "when the Duchess got seven thousand why did you get only two?"

"Well, Aunt Mary, it's all a comparative thing. The Queen of Ruritania gets as much as fifteen thousand, but then, you see, she is royalty. Now, of course, the Duchess of Dexter has a very famous title."

"Plus the O.K. of the late King Edward," speaks up Aunt Mary.

"Of course! But with *our* ancestry, all they would offer me was two thousand." Judy shoots a dirty look at her mother. "That's just the trouble with American ancestry—we all take ourselves seriously because we date back a hundred years or so! The Duchess of Dexter's family goes back centuries, and is really worth money in an advertisement."

Emma looked dazed. Proud of a race as she is, she can't seem to think of a comeback to such definite statistics. But a strange glitter begins to light up the eye of Aunt Mary.

"Judy," she asks thoughtfully, "just exactly who is this Herman Glickman?"

"Well, you see, he is very much interested in charities and it's his job to get the debs to sign up for all the different advertisements, so that they can give the money to their favorite charities."

"Ah, yes—" answers Aunt Mary. "I met a woman at luncheon yesterday who had sold out to silverware, stationery, bathroom fixtures, dressing tables, curtains, cold cream, yeast, radios, lace, and radiators. The only thing the public didn't know about that woman is that she has a lump on her left knee—and all for charity. In fact, she just bought a new Rolls so that she can dash about more quickly from one charity to another."

"But," says Emma, "I don't believe that Judy intends giving her check to charity."

"Of course she does," says Aunt Mary, "only her charity happens to be the promotion of S.A. in Florida."

"She can't go to Florida," says Emma. "That is final! She can't go to Florida without the family and we can't afford to go."

"I have been doing some thinking," says Aunt Mary, "and I have an idea about that." And turning to Judy, she asks, "What's Herman Glickman's address?"

"Mary," gasps Emma, "you wouldn't—"

"If the name of Revell is worth two thousand dollars, the name of van Tassell ought to easily bring five!"

Emma, by this time, is panicky. She goes to Julian, shakes him by the shoulder and says, "Julian, wake up! Wake up! Talk to Mary! She's going to sell the name of van Tassell!"

Julian comes to.

"Where'll she find a taker!" he asks.

Aunt Mary goes over to the console table and picks up a copy of a current magazine. As she glances through it, her eye kindles. The advertising pages are glittering with great names, just like the Social Register—only better than the Register, they have pictures and give details, not only of the lady's pedigree, but even, in some cases, of her plumbing. Aunt Mary enthusiastically hands the magazine to Julian and explains.

Julian takes it in a trembling hand, and after dropping it twice, finally focuses, finds himself staring at the monthly "spread" of a yeast company.

"What's this?" he says, and he reads out, "Famous man about town regulated by yeast!"

"Oh, yes," says Judy, "I forgot about the yeast company, but they only pay five hundred."

"Five hundred for what?" asks Julian.

"For anyone who's been cured by yeast."

"All right," says Julian, "where do I collect?"

Emma seeing the members of her clan dropping from her one by one, begins to see that she is on the losing side of a highly successful revolution. "What is society coming to? Where is the pride? Where is the privilege? Where is the prejudice?"

"Where is Herman Glickman?" asks Aunt Mary. "That is much more to the point."

Judy digs his address out of her pocketbook, and goes off about her afternoon's affairs, which are to end in a scientific demonstration of 100 per cent. S.A. on the American male at tea time, aided by 90 proof substitute for tea.

Emma now faces the two remaining member of her house and begs them not to sell out.

"Don't be silly, Emma," speaks Aunt Mary. "I've suddenly made up my mind to see Florida, which I can't do on my income, in its present state. I haven't had much fun in my old life, and I'm not going to overlook anything from now on! Florida must be divine! I haven't been so thrilled since I discovered Boccaccio at the age of eleven! Julian, get your hat if you're coming with me to Herman's!"

Aunt Mary now picks up the magazine, opens it, turns and addresses her sister.

"Emma, don't be a fool all your life! Here's some magnificent coconut oil, excellent for the hair. All it needs is a life-sized reproduction of that false front of yours to bring it to the attention of every salesgirl that rides the subway. Come on along!"

Emma summons all the van Tassell dignity and pride.

"Never!" she exclaims, "I've never used anything on my hair in all my life."

"Then it's about time you did," says Aunt Mary. "Don't spoil this beautiful morning by holding out on us. Why, I'm all bucked up! I never thought it possible, in this day and age, that our family could mean so much to the community."

"Why, Mary, our family has always been among the first to help in any movement that—"

"Nonsense," says Aunt Mary, "our family hasn't done a darn thing worthy of anybody's notice since great-grandmother carried water to the Continentals on Morristown Heights— And, here is an opportunity to carry oil to those who are fighting just as hard to keep their hair!"

Emma is dazed, but the argument sounds logical.

Aunt Mary continues. "If our family has always been among the first in any great movement of the upper class, how can we lie down now?"

Emma tries to answer but can't think of anything to say.

Aunt Mary thrusts the magazine into her hands and continues, "Consider your duty toward this excellent coconut oil, which has stood the test of half the crowned heads of Europe! Can we of the American Aristocracy do better than follow their lead? Think hard, Emma, because your answer's got to be good!"

Emma thinks as hard as she can, for this last argument pierced clear through her armor of pride and prejudice. After as profound a consideration as Emma's brain is capable of compassing, she speaks.

"Well," she says, "I'll tell you what I'll do. I'll go along with you and I will stop at a drug store and *buy* a bottle of the preparation you speak of, and I'll *use* it, and if tomorrow morning my hair looks improved, I may even consider it my duty, as a van Tassell, to tell the world."

Considering that nothing yet invented by the mind of man could make Emma's hair look *worse* next morning, this is as good as capitulation. And so, keeping her dignity to the last, Emma joins in the expedition that is to boost the house of Revell into the forefront of the winter's social life in Florida.

Author Biographies

DANA AMES (b.?–d.?): No biographical information; possibly a pen name. Ames published a few dozen stories in pulp magazines such as *Snappy Stories, Breezy Stories*, and *Droll Stories* between 1922 and 1926.

KATHERINE BRUSH (1902–1952): Brush was a well-known author of the 1930s and '40s, famous for her short stories and numerous books. Her best-known novels, both made into films, are *Young Man of Manhattan* (1930) and *Red-Headed Woman* (1931). She got her start writing for pulp magazines under her own name and the pen name Barbara Blake before breaking into the slick magazines in the late 1920s.

VIÑA DELMAR (1903–1990): Prolific novelist and author of short stories, plays, and screenplays. She wrote exclusively for *Snappy Stories* from 1922 until that magazine folded in 1927, after which she moved on to the quality slick-paper magazines. Famous for the 1928 bestseller *Bad Girl* and the screenplay for *The Awful Truth*, 1937, for which she was nominated for an Academy Award. Author of over twenty novels.

RUDOLPH FISHER (1897–1934): Doctor, author, and chronicler of the Harlem Renaissance. Author of two novels, a number of important essays, and over a dozen short stories, Fisher is considered a key participant of the Harlem Renaissance. His early death has been attributed to his pioneering work in radiology. The publication of "Common Meter" here reinstates the story's original ending, left off in previous republications.

F. SCOTT FITZGERALD (1896–1940): American novelist most identified with the jazz age. His short stories and early novels captured both the exuberance of the jazz age and, increasingly, his disillusionment with it. "Bernice Bobs Her Hair" is his most well-known flapper story.

ZELDA FITZGERALD (1900–1948): Southern debutante, wife of F. Scott Fitzgerald, and author in her own right. In the 1920s, she gained notoriety as a flapper through Fitzgerald's writing and their well-publicized lifestyle, and as such helped solidify the definition of flapperdom in the public consciousness.

GUY GILPATRIC (1896–1950): Author, journalist, and aviator. Gilpatric is most famous for his serial character Colin Glencannon for the *Saturday Evening Post*, but his earliest stories were aviation themed. Gilpatric is also famous for writing the first book on spearfishing. He died with his wife in 1950 in a suicide pact after she was diagnosed with cancer.

ZORA NEALE HURSTON (1891–1960): Author and member of the Harlem Renaissance whose writing, whether fiction or anthropological non-fiction, covered black life in New York and the southern United States. Her most well-known novel is *Their Eyes Were Watching God* (1937), but she was prolific, writing poetry, fiction, plays, and autobiography.

ANITA LOOS (1888–1981): Screenwriter, author, and playwright most famous for *Gentlemen Prefer Blondes* (1925), a humorous novel whose main character, Lorelei Lee, is a chorus girl, unabashed gold-digger, and arguably literature's most famous flapper. First involved in the film industry in 1912, Loos has well over 100 film writing credits. The influence of writing film scenarios can be seen in the present-tense of "Why Girls Go South."

DOROTHY PARKER (1893–1967): Critic, author, humorist, screenwriter and a member of the infamous Algonquin Round Table—a group of intellectuals and wits associated with the *New Yorker* magazine who lunched at the Algonquin Hotel in midtown Manhattan. Though Parker is most often identified as a humorist, due in part to her acerbic criticism and humorous poetry, she was a serious author with deep political convictions.

DAWN POWELL (1896–1965): Novelist who was born in Ohio but lived most of her life in Greenwich Village. She started writing for pulp magazines, most frequently *Snappy Stories*, in 1921, but graduated to *College Humor* and the *New Yorker* by the early 1930s. Well known for her acerbic novels which chronicle literary life in New York. Though largely out of print at the time of her death, Powell has enjoyed a renaissance over the last few decades. This is the first republication of any of her stories of the 1920s.

GERTRUDE SCHALK aka Toki Schalk (1906–1977): Journalist and author. Though perhaps best known as an editor and columnist for the African American newspaper the *Pittsburgh Courier*, she also wrote prolifically for pulp magazines as well as other African American newspapers. Stories for the latter featured African American characters, unlike those for the pulp magazines. "The Chicago Kid" is just one installment of a series about The Yellow Parrot, an African American nightclub, published in the *National News*.

JOHN WATTS (1900–?): Florida newspaperman and author of a few dozen stories in the snappy pulps throughout the 1920s and 1930s. Originally from Key West, he held newspaper positions in Tampa, New Rochelle, and Washington DC.

Sources

"What Became of the Flapper" by Zelda Fitzgerald was first published in *McCall's*, October 1925

"The Clever Little Fool" by Dana Ames was first published in *Snappy Stories*, June 1926

"Bernice Bobs her Hair" by F. Scott Fitzgerald was first published in the *Saturday Evening Post*, May 1920

"Common Meter" by Rudolph Fisher was first published in the *Pittsburgh Courier*, February 1930

"Something for Nothing" by John Watts was first published in *Snappy Stories*, June 1925

"The Mantle of Whistler" by Dorothy Parker was first published in the *New Yorker*, August 1928

"Night Club" by Katharine Brush was first published in *Harper's Magazine*, September 1927

"The Chicago Kid" by Gertrude Schalk was first published in the *National News*, March 1932

"Not the Marrying Kind" by Dawn Powell was first published in *Snappy Stories*, March 1927

"Thou Shalt Not Killjoy" by Viña Delmar was first published in *Snappy Stories*, December 1923

"The Bride of Ballyhoo" by Guy Gilpatric was first published in *College Humor*, January 1929

"Money Junk" by Zora Neale Hurston was first published in the *Pittsburgh Courier*, March 1927

"Why Girls Go South" by Anita Loos was first published in *Harper's Bazaar*, January 1926

Essential Pushkin Collection

Part of the Pushkin Collection, the Essentials are specially curated selections of the most vital and thrilling short stories and essays by classic writers. These collections are handpicked from around the world – from Russia to Japan, Brazil to Poland – and boast new translations and stylishly illustrated covers. They serve as introductions to icons of world literature, and each one is desirable, enthralling, and nothing short of essential.

The Pushkin Collection of paperbacks, complete with French flaps, is designed to be as satisfying as possible to hold and to enjoy. Each book is typeset in Monotype Baskerville, based on the transitional English serif type-face designed in the mid-eighteenth century by John Baskerville. They are litho-printed on Munken Premium White Paper and notch-bound by the independently owned printer TJ Books in Padstow, Cornwall.